The Night Riders
of
Harpers Ferry

The Night Riders
of
Harpers Ferry

by Kathleen Ernst

 White Mane Publishing Company, Inc.

Sketches by Susan Fries.

This White Mane Publishing Company, Inc. publication was printed by:
Beidel Printing House, Inc.
63 West Burd Street
Shippensburg, PA 17257 USA

In respect for the scholarship contained herein, the acid-free paper used in this book meets the guidelines for permanence and durability of the Committee on Production Guidelines for Book Longevity of the Council on Library Resources.

For a complete list of available publications, please write:
White Mane Publishing Company, Inc.
P. O. Box 152
Shippensburg, PA 17257-0152 USA

Library of Congress Cataloging-in-Publication Data

Ernst, Kathleen, 1959–
     The night riders of Harpers Ferry / by Kathleen Ernst.
          p.   cm.
     Summary: During the Civil War, a seventeen-year-old Union soldier must adjust to army life, with the additional complications peculiar to the region where the Shenandoah and Potomac Rivers come together at Harpers Ferry, West Virginia.
          ISBN 1-57249-013-6 (alk. paper)
          1.   United States--History--Civil War, 1861-1865--Juvenile fiction. 2. Antietam, Battle of, Md., 1862--Fiction. [1. United States--History--Civil War, 1862-1865--Fiction. 2. Antietam, Battle of, Md., 1862--Fiction.] I. Title.
PZ7.E7315N1   1996
[Fic]--dc20   96-2524
                                                                     CIP
                                                                      AC

edication

This book is dedicated
to the memory of
Lewis Maitland Johnston.
He was a good man.

CONTENTS

Chapter One 1

Chapter Two 7

Chapter Three 16

Chapter Four 27

Chapter Five 35

Chapter Six 49

Chapter Seven 60

Chapter Eight 69

Chapter Nine 77

Chapter Ten 92

Chapter Eleven 99

Chapter Twelve 107

Chapter Thirteen 116

Chapter Fourteen 124

Epilogue 136

Author's Note 137

ACKNOWLEDGMENTS

Heartfelt appreciation is extended to the many people who helped make this book possible, including all those who had the vision to preserve Harpers Ferry and the C & O Canal in the National Park Service system. Thanks go to Maryellen Lowe, Dennis Trudell, and Rich Gillespie, who took the time to read and comment on early drafts; Marion Dane Bauer and my friends at the SCBWI-WI, who provided encouragement when I needed it; Dr. Richard Haney and Dr. Linda Ziegahn, who were open-minded enough to consider this project suitable for my masters' program; and Dr. Martin Gordon and Dr. Diane Gordon, who were willing to take the manuscript on. Gordon Gay, Chief of Interpretive Services, C & O Canal National Historical Park; Bruce Noble, Park Historian, Harpers Ferry National Park; Steve Wright, Curator, Civil War Library and Museum; and Debbi Parish of American Heritage Engravings all helped me locate illustrations for the book.

I'm particularly indebted to two friends and kindred spirits, Juilene Osborne McKnight and Eileen Charbonneau. Juilene believed in the book when it was no more than a wisp of an idea, and generously shared her mentor. Eileen dispensed editorial wisdom and Virginia hospitality with equal generosity, and patiently guided the process from rough draft to finished product. Eileen, thank you.

My family has believed in me and been supportive of my writing for many years, and I'm grateful for their patience and faith. Thank you all: Stephanie Ernst, Barbara Ernst, Michael MacGeorge, Priscilla Angotti, and Henry Ernst.

And finally, thank you, Scott, for wanting me to have time to write.

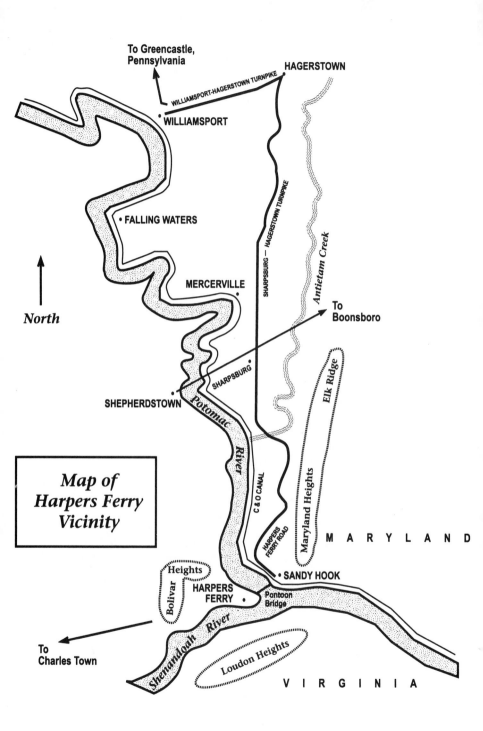

Map of
Harpers Ferry
Vicinity

CHAPTER ONE

I never saw Mahalia cry. I met her the day she came plum close to drowning, which would have set most women to tears. But not Mahalia.

I am used to weeping women, having been surrounded by too many for all of my seventeen years. I have six sisters back home, in New York. They cried like the heavens opened the day I left with the cavalry regiment I'd up and joined. Ma was crying too, saying "My boy," over and over, which made me want to get on with it even quicker.

Betsy Lee Thornton cried a lot too. She was pretty as a field of violets in May. She wept pretty too, the afternoon she told me she didn't want to marry me after all, like she was the one getting her heart torn out and not the other way around.

But Mahalia never cried. And she had more reason than most.

The first time I saw Mahalia Sutter she was standing on a rock in the Potomac River. I was riding on the Maryland side, toward the army pontoon bridge that would get me across the rapids to Harpers Ferry where my regiment was bivouacked. It was a wild, beautiful place, that riverside coming down to the junction of the Shenandoah River. The cliffs of Maryland Heights rose a thousand feet straight above, with room for just one slope-hugging dirt road, and the strip of land along the C & O Canal, in between. Across the Potomac, Harpers Ferry clung to its point of land. Beyond the river junction, Loudon Heights rolled along. Those two rivers cut right through the mountains. I'd never seen anything like it.

The Potomac races over rocky ledges along that stretch where I was riding, as if it can't wait to meet the Shenandoah. Fishermen pull shad and bluebacks from the eddies along the bank. Sometimes boys jump out to boulders farther from shore with their poles, daring each other, looking for excitement as much as supper.

That afternoon, Mahalia was standing on a rock about a hundred feet from shore, so far from the next closest rock I reckoned it was quite a jump for her. She was barefoot, and had on a mustard-colored dress—plain, hemmed up above the ankles for easy walking, not hooped and silken like the dresses Betsy Lee wore. Mahalia was looking downstream.

I nudged my mare Cinder along, so I could see the girl's face. She didn't notice. She was very still, staring at the water.

A better man probably would have called out to her. But she wouldn't have heard over the rushing water, I reckon. I slid my sketchpad from the saddlebag—my personal one, not the one I used for making maps for Colonel Davis. I flipped past all the drawings I'd made of Betsy Lee, and found my pencil stub.

She was some younger than me, I figured. My pencil drew a slim girl, with a long braid the color of cornsilk and a sharp nose. I made another mark or two, trying to capture her expression, so strange and empty.

When I looked back up—she was gone. Shock punched me in the gut. Then I saw a bit of that ugly yellow dress in the water.

What happened next came so fast it's hard to put down right. I slid off Cinder and scrambled to the shore. I got another glimpse of her dress. She was upstream from me a few yards, but tumbling fast, hitting against rocks all the time. I knew better than to jump in after her. I'm a good swimmer, but the current in those rapids is powerful strong.

There was a rock just out from shore, close in line to her path, and a sycamore tree on the bank spread its branches down close to the water. I jumped out to that rock and flattened down. I'm lanky, and I stretched my arm as far as I could. But I'd heard how drowning people can drag their rescuers down, so I kept a good hold of one of those branches too.

For an instant I thought she'd gone under for good. Then I caught sight of her hair. Her body slammed against the rock I was on and I grabbed mightily. I caught hold of her arm, but it got wrenched out of my hand. That's when I gave up all figuring and just plunged in after her.

The cold hit hard, and the current caught me like I was a twig. But I got a good hold on her skirt, and I didn't aim to let go. The two of us tumbled over another rock. It caught me in the shin so hard I yelped and got a mouthful of water. On the next slam I managed to brace myself against the rock and hold us there long enough to get my arm around her.

There weren't many choices left. I launched out for shore, dragging the girl along and fighting the current with one arm. My wool uniform weighed about a bale. Fortunately we got bounced closer toward the bank, and I was mighty thankful for that.

Halfway there the girl came to life and started thrashing around. "Be still!" I croaked. My lungs were about to burst when I felt gravel. I stumbled into a calm backwater where the water shallowed out. I dragged the girl 'til her head and shoulders were up on the bank before my strength gave out. We were both coughing and spitting like two beached catfish.

"You're safe now," I panted.

"Damnation !" It was gasped out so ragged I could hardly be sure I'd heard right. But I had.

Well, I don't mind saying I was shocked. It had been a terrorizing experience, but I'd never heard a girl say such a thing. She crawled up on the muddy bank, and I just stared after her.

Before I could gather my wits I heard a shout. An old man hobbled toward us. "Sweet Jesus," he quavered. "Sweet Jesus, I saw it all. Thought you were goners."

I stood, which was a chore with my high boots and uniform soaking wet. "I thought so myself," I managed, and then looked down at the girl I'd almost drowned myself to rescue, and gotten cursed at for my trouble. She was still gasping, but pushed herself up on her knees, which I took for a good sign. Her dress was plastered to her and I couldn't help noticing she wasn't quite as young as I had taken her for, maybe even seventeen like me. Her hair was plastered down too, that braid undone. Tendrils draped around her head like eelgrass.

I was almost afraid to speak to her, but my mama raised a gentleman. It wasn't proper to pull someone from a river and then walk away. "Miss, are you well?"

She coughed once more, then heaved her shoulders. "Yes," she said, in a tone different from the brazen one I'd heard before. She sounded disappointed. Defeated.

The old man didn't give me much time to ponder. "Mahalia Sutter, what come over you?" he scolded. And to me, "She's been jumping rocks on this river all her life. Swims like a fish, besides. I can't figure what happened."

"I just slipped, Mr. Timmerman," she said quietly. I offered my arm. She took it and heaved to her feet. "I was careless."

"The name's Francis Timmerman," the old man said to me, holding out his hand. "You're quite a hero, young man."

I have to say "hero" wasn't a word that had ever been thrown my way. It sounded pretty good, even coming from a barefoot old man with a pocket full of worms. Besides, some folks thereabouts didn't use the word in connection with any soldier wearing Yankee blue, even if Maryland was still officially in the Union.

"Solomon Hargreave," I introduced myself. "Eighth New York Cavalry. It's a pleasure to make your acquaintance, sir. Right now, I better be seeing Miss Sutter home."

"Fine thing, fine thing," Mr. Timmerman nodded.

"I can walk." Mahalia drew herself up straight, although she didn't let her eyes meet mine. "I thank you kindly for pulling me out of the river, Mr. Hargreave." With that she turned and started walking away.

Well, like I said, my mama raised me to be a gentleman, and I wasn't about to have a young lady walking home alone after near to drowning in the Potomac River. Even though it was only the first of September, the breeze was a bit chill against our wet clothes. And there were hazards this close to the Virginia border, bands of hard-riding Rebel bushwhackers who splashed across the Potomac after dark. Besides, I admit I was pretty baffled by Mahalia. I'd go plum crazy trying to figure her out if I let her walk away.

"I won't hear of it," I said, real firm. "I'll fetch my horse and take you home."

I thought she was going to refuse. Then she glanced at Mr. Timmerman, who was eagerly watching the exchange, and seemed to think better of it. She nodded.

Cinder was browsing where I'd left her. I picked up my hat, and slid the sketchpad back in the saddlebag, before mounting and trotting back. I gave Mahalia a hand and she reluctantly swung up behind the saddle.

Mr. Timmerman was grinning as I turned the mare's head around. "He'll have the story all over Sandy Hook by tomorrow, I don't doubt," I said. Sandy Hook was the tiny village just downstream of the Potomac and Shenandoah junction.

"I'm sure that'd please you right fine," Mahalia snapped. The submissive girl was gone again.

"That's not what I meant," I began, but decided against explaining further. "Where do you live, anyway?"

"Lock Thirty-Six."

It took me a full minute to figure out that address. But I wasn't about to ask her to explain.

CHAPTER TWO

Where the Potomac drops off rapidly, like at that stretch near Harpers Ferry, boat pens called "locks" are needed in the canal to account for the drop in terrain. Each lock was numbered, and needed a keeper. Lock Thirty-Six was about two miles upstream from us.

I nudged Cinder over the slope and we trotted onto the towpath, a flat dusty trail with the Potomac River on one side and the Chesapeake and Ohio Canal on the other. The canal company doesn't allow any traffic on the towpath except its own mule drivers, but the army generally ignores that rule. The canal stretches from Cumberland, Maryland, all the way to Washington D.C.—almost two hundred miles. It was built back in the 1830s, to haul cargo. Now the Union army uses it to float coal downstream for the government. The Rebs had tried to damage the canal more than once in the year and a half since the war began, but so far, hadn't done any permanent harm.

"Does your father keep the lock?" I asked.

"My father's dead."

She wasn't a girl for easy conversation, that was sure. I owled up then myself and we made the rest of the trip in silence.

7

The lockkeeper's house was a two-story brick building on the Potomac side of the canal. Situated in the curve of a deep bend in the river, it was sheltered from flood danger by a high brick guard wall. There was about an acre cleared around it, with a stable and a large garden beyond. A couple of chickens were scratching in the yard, and two tow-headed kids were playing in the dirt close by. There were weeds in the garden and loose shingles on the stable and a piece of fence fallen down. On the whole the place didn't look well tended. I knew that look, though. My pa died when I was still in knee pants, and our farm declined considerable before my ma sold the place and we moved to town.

Mahalia slid down. "Thanks for the ride," she said quickly.

Before she could disappear, a woman came out the front door. "Mahalia?" she called, shielding her eyes from the sun. "Where've you been?" Her gaze found me. "Who's that? Bring him in."

Caught between us, I reckon Mahalia didn't know what to say or do. She looked over her shoulder at me and shrugged. I slid down and looped Cinder's reins over the hitching rail.

"Land sakes, what happened?" the older woman cried as we got closer. I guess we did look a sight. I'd been trying to flesh out some, but being soaked didn't improve my still-skinny frame. And my black hair had grown over my collar, and looked worse wet than dry.

"I was fishing, Ma, and slipped. This here is Solomon Hargreave. He happened along and plucked me out."

I hadn't seen sign of a fishing pole anywhere near Mahalia, but I didn't mention that. Mrs. Sutter didn't give me much chance, anyway. She was clucking, shooing us inside like a worried hen with a pair of chicks gone astray.

The sitting room wasn't fancy like the parlor at Betsy Lee's house. I could see on through to the kitchen, where another flax-haired girl was stirring a kettle on the big black cookstove. The smell of stewed chicken hung in the air.

Mahalia disappeared upstairs, and I was left to talk to her mother. She seemed kind, if a bit dazed. But I knew that look, too—of a woman who worked too hard, birthed too many babies, and lost heart along the way. My own mother didn't wear that look. My mother liked to take charge. But I'd seen it often, in the neighbor-women back in Millersville.

When Mahalia came downstairs, I got another shock. She was wearing trousers, without even an overskirt, like girls wear when they parade around as daughters of a regiment. A man's shirt was tucked in at her waist.

Mrs. Sutter frowned. "Mahalia, where's your other dress?"

"No sense in me putting on Sunday best unless you or Phoebe want to swing sluice gates," Mahalia said. "I'm going to see if she needs kindling."

"Mahalia, you are not attending to your guest," Mrs. Sutter said, as if I was a grand Sunday caller. "Mr. Hargreave needs some dry clothes."

That caught my attention. "Oh, no thank you, ma'am," I said. "I have to go—"

"You will stay to dinner," she decreed calmly. "It's not every day Mahalia has a gentleman caller. Mahalia, the clothes."

Mahalia cringed at her words. "I don't think he—"

"Corbin's will do. I don't expect him tonight."

Mahalia looked like she wanted to say something, but then gave in and fetched the clothes. I went upstairs to change. Ten minutes later our wet things were draped out in the kitchen to dry, giving off the powerful smell of wet wool, and I sat down to supper with the Sutter clan.

Mrs. Sutter sat at one end of a long trestle table, and there were kids on benches up one side and down the other. There were five besides Mahalia and her older sister, Phoebe, and none looked a day over twelve. One, still in diapers, gurgled in a cradle by Mrs. Sutter's chair.

There was one more place set at the head of the table. I looked at it when Phoebe commenced passing the food.

"Mama always keeps a plate for Mr. Sutter," she said, as if it was nothing out of the ordinary to set the table for a dead man. "Would you care for some peas?"

Phoebe looked like Mahalia, in some ways: she had the same yellow hair, and the same sharp nose. In other ways she couldn't have been more different. She was wearing a pretty dress, held out with one of those hoopskirt contraptions. Her hair was up and tidy, with one careful curl beside each cheek. She talked dainty and blushed and minded her manners. For all the ruder surroundings, she reminded me more than a bit of Betsy Lee.

"If you don't mind me asking," I said, "are you two twins?" It was funny to see two girls so alike and yet so different.

Mahalia stared at her plate. "No, but we're only eleven months apart. My brother Corbin and I were born first. We're twins."

I noticed the younger ones staring like they weren't sure what to think of me. "My name is Solomon," I said, as friendly as I could.

"Mahalia, didn't you make proper introductions?" Phoebe scolded mildly, and pointed out the children one by one. Clem, Howie, Rose, Lizzie. And Thomas is the baby.

"We're honored that you could dine with us, Mr. Hargreave," Phoebe went on sweetly, passing me a platter of biscuits. "My sister was fortunate that you came to her rescue."

I felt my cheeks turn red, hoping the word "hero" wouldn't come up again. "It was nothing," I mumbled.

"You're in the cavalry?"

That I was proud of. "Yes I am, Miss Sutter. Company H, Eighth New York Cavalry Regiment."

"Are you stationed on Maryland Heights?"

"Harpers Ferry."

"Corbin's in the cavalry," Howie announced, kicking the table leg.

I smiled at him. "Really? What regiment?"

"Howie, be quiet," Mahalia said. She startled me, since she hadn't had a word to say since I'd come back downstairs. I stared at her. For the first time, she looked me square in the eye. "My brother crossed the river." She threw the words down on the table like a dare.

Crossed the river. I knew what that meant in this cantankerous border state. Her brother was riding for the Confederacy. I was wearing the clothes of my enemy.

Everybody got real quiet. Mrs. Sutter sagged in her chair, looking unhappy.

Then Lizzie knocked a plate of stewed chicken on the floor. At the same minute I heard a strange horn call outside. Mahalia jumped to her feet.

"Mahalia, where are you going?" Mrs. Sutter asked.

"To get the lock, Ma."

"Don't leave the table while your caller is here. Your father must be outside. He'll tend to it."

Well, hearing her speak of her husband like he was still alive froze me to the bench. Mahalia didn't even turn from the door. "Pa isn't going to get it, Ma," she said simply, and went on outside.

No one else even seemed to notice. The kids had gone back to their supper, shoveling their food and whining for more and generally causing a ruckous. Phoebe carried an empty bowl into the kitchen.

"I'll go help Mahalia," I said, which was foolish, since I had no idea how to work a lock. But I couldn't stand to be in that house for another minute. I bolted after Mahalia.

Outside, the canalboat was just easing up to the lock in front of the house. "Hey, lockee!" a man on deck cried. "Lock on through!" Mahalia waved.

I'd passed canalboats before, but I'd never seen one locked through. For a moment I forgot about the crazy family I'd stumbled into.

The boat was about ninety feet long, with a mule shed at one end and a cabin at the other. Two little girls were sitting on the cabin roof, with their bare feet dangling over the sides. They had ropes tied around their waists to prevent accidents—a good idea, I thought, in light of my own afternoon's experience. Out in front, on the path, a barefoot boy was unhitching the two-mule team that towed the boat along.

The boatman eased his vessel into the lock, which took some skill, because it barely fit. Its fourteen or so feet width cleared each lock wall by no more than three inches.

Once it was bobbing inside the lock, the boatman threw Mahalia a rope. She wound it quickly around a snubbing post, carefully eyeing the play so the boat had enough momentum to clear the upstream gate, but not enough to crash through the lower gate or snap the post. That done, she threw her body's weight against the swing beam to pull the upper sluice gate closed. Then she ran to the lower gate and pulled it open. As the water drained from the lock, the boat slowly lowered to the level of the canal downstream.

I was impressed, I have to say. I'd almost forgotten that she was wearing those godawful trousers. Then I saw her gesturing at me impatiently. With some embarrassment, I realized she wanted help. Quickly, I unwound the line from the rope-scarred post and tossed it back to the laughing boatman. The mules were hitched back to the line. With a wave, the captain turned downstream and the boat continued on its way. Mahalia waited until he was clear and then began tugging the lower gate closed again. I ran to help her push the gate's swing beam back in place.

"That's tricky business," I said. "You handle this alone?"

Mahalia glared. "You going to report us to the company?"

"No! What would I do that for?"

"Because they don't know my father's dead. If they knew, they'd hire another man."

And the Sutter family would be turned out. "I don't have any reason to tell. It's no concern of mine. But..." I hesitated, knowing how prickly this strange girl could be, "can you handle it? Don't you need help?"

"I do all right. Sometimes Clem—he's eleven—helps. If a boatman handles the rope, Clem and Howie can do it by themselves, now. The boatmen, they've been good to us. We're supposed to have them cleared in eight minutes, but no one's said a word if it goes over."

"It just don't seem right, for a girl—"

"What do you know!" She balled her hands into tight fists. "Look, I don't need you telling me what's right! You don't know what's right for my family. You don't know what it's like to have your pa dead—"

"Yes I do!" I blazed back. "My father's been dead since I was nine."

That shut her up, but she didn't apologize.

I hesitated, but couldn't help asking, "Did your mama mention your father so I wouldn't know? That he's dead, I mean?"

Mahalia gave me a hard look. "No. She don't always know it herself. Pa Sutter was my stepfather, so it's the second time she's been widowed. She's had a hard time."

"When did he die?"

"A year ago. At Manassas."

At Manassas, the bloody battlefield the Northerners call Bull Run. Mr. Sutter had been in the army, then.

"And so you don't have to ask," she added coldly, "he was wearing blue."

Well, this girl had a talent for rendering me speechless. Her stepfather had been in the Union army. I thought about her brother, who was riding for the Confederacy. I thought about Phoebe, who seemed to want to pretend that none of the trouble was happening. I thought about her mother, who was not quite right in the head. And I thought about pulling a girl who could "swim like a fish" from the Potomac.

It was more than I could take into account. "I best be getting back across the river," I said. I didn't owe these people anything, did I? Besides, Mahalia sure didn't want me around. That was plain.

We went inside long enough for me to change. My uniform was still clammy in spots, but Phoebe had brushed off the worst of the mud. I laid Corbin's things out on the bed and clattered downstairs, eager to be away.

Mrs. Sutter was in the sitting room. Mahalia was coming in with an armload of firewood. "I thank you kindly for dinner, Miss Sutter, Mrs. Sutter," I said in my most polite voice.

Before they could answer Phoebe came out of the kitchen, wiping her hands on a towel. "Oh Mr. Hargreave, must you leave so soon?" She pouted. "Well, we know you must attend to your duties. Good evening."

"Mahalia, you may see your caller off," Mrs. Sutter said. "Mr. Hargreave, we will look forward to seeing you again."

Mahalia followed me out only because she didn't want to be contrary to her mother, I could tell. I mounted quickly. She surprised me by running a hand down Cinder's withers. "You've got a good horse."

"Yes, I'm lucky," I stammered. It was the first pleasant thing she'd said to me. Besides, she'd hit a vulnerable point, for I am powerful proud of Cinder. "And you've got a good eye for horseflesh."

"Oh, I know horses," she said, stepping back.

I'm ashamed to say that once I was on the towpath, I kneed Cinder into a quick canter. I wanted to show off—either me or the mare, I'm not rightly sure which. But it was a wasted show. When I glanced over my shoulder, Mahalia had already gone inside.

Canalboat settling gently in Lock 42. This shows the type of lock Mahalia tended in this story.

C & O Canal National Historical Park,
National Park Service

Maryland Heights, Harpers Ferry
This period sketch shows the C & O Canal and towpath near the spot where Solomon first met Mahalia. Note the three artillery pieces beneath the cliffs.

J. D. Woodward

CHAPTER THREE

Showing off on the mare was not only wasted effort, it was stupid. Although Captain de Vries had formed our regiment a year before, in 1861, we'd only gotten issued horses a month earlier. The government in its wisdom had kept us on foot until then. We'd been drilling powerful hard in the past few weeks, and even been out patrolling the railroad toward Charles Town. But truth to tell, we were still getting used to actually having horses.

We had a new colonel, too, who came with the mounts. Benjamin F. Davis we hadn't expected: a Southerner, raised in Mississippi, who had two brothers serving in the Eleventh Mississippi Infantry Regiment, Confederate army. He'd gone to the United States Military Academy at West Point, and knew his business. Still, some of the boys still gaped like dying fish when Colonel Davis opened his mouth and that drawl slid out.

He was probably waiting for me, so I kept Cinder at a trot as we followed the towpath, then crossed the new pontoon bridge. The army built it to replace the bridge destroyed by the Rebels the year before. The ruins of that old bridge still thrust up like some bony skeleton out of the rapids.

16

It was getting dark by the time I got across the river. The lamplighter was making his rounds. It should have been a peaceable scene, but Harpers Ferry was a funny town. It was both the most beautiful and the most desolate place I'd ever seen, at the same time.

Before the war the splendid scenery attracted tourists. The town was also so busy with industry that people said the smell of coal burning was always in the air, and the sound of hammers was like to drive a man crazy. There was a textile mill and a flour mill along the Shenandoah, and a huge Federal armory along the Potomac banks. The B & O railroad goes through the mountain passes there, and meets the Winchester and Potomac branch at the point, which brought all kinds of traffic.

But that was before John Brown tried to start a Negro insurrection there in 1859, and got hanged for his trouble. That was before the war got started. Since, Harpers Ferry's been taken back and forth by the Rebels and the Yankees like some bone two dogs are worrying over. That railroad's vital. Both armies want to control it.

By the time the Eighth New York Cavalry arrived in August 1862, most of the townsfolk had fled. A group of ragged runaway slaves, called contrabands, had pitched a forlorn camp in one of the empty yards. The railroad bridge had been burned and repaired more than once, and most of the arsenal and industry buildings were either burned or shut down. Blackened ruins were on every side, and when it rained, the town still stank of smoke. The few civilians left slunk wary through the streets. It was a ghostly place.

Almost two thousand Federal infantry were stationed in Harpers Ferry, most of them camped out on Bolivar Heights, the hill rising back from the town. We'd found the Twelfth Illinois Cavalry there too, a few companies of Rhode Island horsemen, and some Marylanders called Coles Cavalry. It was the first time we'd felt like real cavalry. Colonel Dixon Miles, who commanded the Federal garrison at Harpers Ferry, was mostly set to keeping the Rebel bushwhackers from harassing the B & O. The "Railroad Brigade," people called us.

That evening I had to report to Colonel Davis. After tending to Cinder I found the colonel in the abandoned house on High Street where he and some other officers were staying. It struck me odd to see saddlebags and boots and sabers in what had once been the sitting room, and maps tacked to the walls where pictures might have once hung.

"Hargreave! I was beginning to wonder if you'd run into trouble," Colonel Davis greeted me. He was a handsome man, about thirty years old, with a beard and mustache I admired. I noticed he didn't in particular look worried. I tried to believe that was because he had faith in me.

"Not any real trouble, sir. I did the drawings you wanted."

"Good! Let's see."

I handed him my sketches. He cleared the dining room table to spread them out. "Corliss!" he called. "Come take a look."

Major Corliss commanded a squadron of the Rhode Island Cavalry. We called his troopers the "college cavaliers," because most of them were three-month volunteers from Dartmouth College in New Hampshire or Norwich University in Vermont. I suspect, though, we also called them that to stiff up our own confidence. We New Yorkers were pretty green, as cavalrymen, and it was nice to find some greener than ourselves.

When Major Corliss came into the room, Colonel Davis introduced me. "I found Private Hargreave down by the river junction last week, making a sharp drawing," he explained. "I decided to put his abilities to work for us. He's been getting a look at the terrain on the Maryland side. Show him what you've got, Hargreave."

I tried to not show how proud I was at being singled out, and having two officers waiting for my report! "Well, sirs, this shows Sandy Hook, below the junction. You had wondered about that reputed ford, but the rapids... here... would make it impossible. This next one shows the road up to Maryland Heights. Not the one the army uses, but the old track the townfolk still use—"

"That looks like a forty-five percent grade," Corliss frowned. "The topo maps don't show it to be that severe."

"Well, sir, this is accurate. I think the problem is your map." I bent over it. "This shows only the main road. But the charcoal crews have cut their own traces all over the ridge. Rough, but passable. There's one here... and another here." With my finger, I traced a number of tracks giving access to the steep cliffs of Maryland Heights, and the long ridge known as Elk Ridge which extended north from the heights.

We went on from there. It got dark, and an aide brought a couple of oil lamps. Major Corliss lit a cigar and offered one to the colonel, who declined in favor of his pipe. I liked being there, being listened to, smelling the tobacco smoke and talking important war business. Me! Solomon Hargreave, the skinny boy from New York who never was much use to anybody, who never fit in. Maybe, I thought as we finished, I'll be a credit to the cavalry after all.

Then Colonel Davis asked me another question. "What detained you, Hargreave? You didn't run into any bushwhackers, did you?"

I was tempted to lie. The Southern irregulars mostly stayed on the Virginia side of the Potomac, harassing any Yankees they could find and stealing from Union sympathizers. But lately they'd been making bolder raids into Maryland. I longed to say, 'Yes, Colonel, but I dispatched them right quick. Killed three of them and sent the rest running for their lives—'

But my mama didn't raise a liar. "No, sir," I said with regret, then added reluctantly, "I saw a girl fall into the river. I pulled her out, and seeing as how she was soaked and all, I took her home. Then her mama pressed me into staying for supper...." I trailed off, seeing the two men exchange an amused look. "I'm sorry, sir."

"No need, Hargreave," the colonel said tolerantly. He leaned back in his chair and propped his boots on the table, crossing his ankles. "It's hard to protest a girl's mama. You haven't had much adventure yet. Might as well find some romance. What's your young lady friend's name?"

The colonel had gotten the wrong idea, that was sure. But I didn't know how to get out of answering. "Mahalia Sutter, sir."

The name got more of a reaction than I expected. The amusement disappeared from his face, and the front legs of his chair banged back on the floor. "Sutter?"

"Yes sir."

The Colonel looked at Major Corliss. "Augustus, do you suppose...?"

Corliss shrugged, looking interested, and Colonel Davis looked back to me. "Is this young lady's father a lockkeeper?"

I couldn't imagine why he wanted to know. "He was sir, but he's dead. Mahalia—the young lady—mostly tends it now." Then I burst out, "But I promised not to tell that, sir! The family needs the job, and the company doesn't know Mr. Sutter's dead."

"I'm not interested in the young lady's father, I'm interested in her brother. Did she happen to mention her brother to you? Corbin Sutter?"

"The name came up, sir." I hesitated, then dared ask, "What is this about, Colonel?

"Hargreave, we've had reports about a Reb guerilla named Corbin Sutter."

"A raider?" I stammered, like a schoolboy. "I got the idea he was regular cavalry." We Yankee horsemen offered the Reb cavalry grudging respect, because they could ride like nobody's business. But the bushwhackers were little more than thieves.

"From what civilians have told us, he's the leader of a band of riders. They call themselves the Loudon County Scouts—"

"The Loudon County Scouts!"

"You've heard of them."

"Well, yes sir, all the boys have. A fellow in the blacksmith's shop, he said they shot in the windows of Unionists at night. And there's this Negro woman, she sells pies, she said they were like ghosts, disappearing so fast a body couldn't see it." The old woman also said the Scouts could ride circles around us if we were on the edge of a cliff. I didn't figure I should repeat that to these two officers.

Colonel Davis grunted. "They've earned a reputation. They've stayed mostly in Virginia, but Corbin and a few of the others have homes in Maryland—"

"Had, you mean?" Major Corliss interrupted.

"That's the question." The colonel looked me square in the eye. "Hargreave, we've had reports indicating that Corbin Sutter was killed in a skirmish last week. What did you hear at the Sutter place?"

I took in that news and tried hard to remember things rightly. "He wasn't discussed in much detail, sir. His mama said something about not expecting him tonight, though." I didn't feel a need to mention I'd borrowed Corbin Sutter's clothes. Not just a Confederate cavalryman, but leader of a gang of partisans!

"Think hard, Hargreave," Corliss pressed. "It's important."

I rubbed my forehead, trying to understand.

"The boy is something of a local hero, among the Reb sympathizers," Colonel Davis explained. "Those raiders have been hard on us. It would be good for our side's morale to know Corbin Sutter is gone. It's in the Secessionists' best interests to maintain otherwise as long as possible, even if he is dead. Do you recall any other hints? Was the family mourning?"

Now, that was a particularly good question. In my sights, none of those Sutter women acted normal that afternoon. But grieving a new-lost son? Who could tell? "I don't know, sir," I allowed after a long moment, when the only sound in the room was a pesky moth battering at the lamp. "I mean, there was no black crape on the door, or anything. Best as I recollect, the only thing said was that he wasn't expected that night. And his sister told me he had crossed the river. But nothing else."

Colonel Davis got up abruptly and fetched a bottle of whiskey from the sideboard. I hoped he was going to offer me some, but he only poured two glasses. After pushing one toward Major Corliss, he ran a hand through his hair. "I tell you what, Augustus," he said. "Jeb Stuart's cavalry has made a mockery of the Union. There's not much I can do about that. But I'll be damned if I'll let some local rabble make a mockery of me and my troops."

Those dire words sounded so queer spoken in Major Davis's soft Southern drawl that I felt a shiver skitter along my backbone. I got the feeling he had forgotten me, standing silent in the shadows. I held my tongue, wanting to hear more.

But the mounted provost guard clattered by the window on patrol, and the mood was broken. "Hargreave."

"Yes sir?"

"Are you welcome to return to the Sutter house?"

Welcome by who? Mahalia? Or her mother? "Well, her mama did say to call again." I didn't add that her mama was not quite right in the head.

"I want you to do something for me. Go back there. Visit again. Learn what you can about Corbin Sutter. Will you do that?"

Well, I don't mind saying I had mixed feelings about that. "You mean... to spy?"

He smiled. "Nothing so dramatic. Find out what you can. I want to know if Corbin Sutter is dead or alive. If you can find out more about the Loudon County Scouts, so much the better. Fall in and drill with the rest for the next few days. But I'll dismiss you from afternoon drill again on Friday. No, I'll dismiss you all day. I'd like you to make a few more sketches for me, too."

I made as sharp a salute as I knew how. But before I got to the door something made me turn around. "Colonel—Mr. Sutter was in the Union army. He was killed at Bull Run last year. That is one sorry family."

I felt foolish as soon as the words were out of my mouth, for I can't rightly say what I expected him to answer. But he just looked down at his whiskey. "This war has made many sorry families," he said, and drained what was left in the glass.

Military regulations are confusing at times. After I left the colonel, I wasn't sure if I had to report in with the captain of my company or not. To be safe, I decided to let him know I was back.

Captain de Vries had been an attorney before the war started. Folks back home in Millersville said he'd decided to raise a cavalry regiment because he wanted to stump for office, and thought military glory would win him votes. It seemed like a mighty gamble to me.

That night he did nothing to earn my future ballot. "Well Hargreave?"

"Uh, I just thought I should report in, sir. That I'm back, I mean."

He stood on the front step of the house where he was staying. He's a short man, and I reckon uncomfortable about it, because he often maneuvers so he can talk down to people. "Did you report to Colonel Davis?"

"Yes sir. I was just there."

"Then you have no need of me. This was his errand, not mine." Before I could salute he turned away and went back inside.

It was a short walk to quarters. Like the officers, we soldiers were settled into an abandoned house. Unlike them, we didn't have any decent furniture and bottles of whiskey and oil lamps. We had piles of straw in empty rooms to spread our blankets on, and smoky candle-lanterns to play cards or write letters by. Peanut shells and dirty socks were scattered about. Comrades piled in so close it was common to wake up with someone's elbow in my eye.

I found some of my messmates playing dice in a corner of our upstairs room. My friend Randolph McAllister looked up. "Hey Sol, come join us."

Before I could answer, Gillis cut in. "Naw. This is a *man's* game." A buddy of his, called Rusty because of his hair, added, "No ladies allowed."

I didn't know exactly what that meant, and I was too tired to look for a fight. I went and lay down on my blanket by one wall. After a couple of minutes Randolph sat down beside me. "What kept you?"

"I was talking to Colonel Davis." I tried to say it quiet-like, so it didn't seem like I was bragging. I angled my head toward the dice players. "What's with them?"

In the shadows, Randolph looked sheepish. "Aw, nothin'. Some of them are just beefed because Colonel Davis let you off of drill."

Captain de Vries was too, I thought. "Are you?"

"Naw." Randolph grinned. "Hey, Sol! I went up the hill afterwards and found that old woman who sells pies. I got an apple pie for fifty cents. I saved you a piece. Want it?"

Randolph and his pies. He was a chubby kid who missed his mama's cooking like some of the guys missed their sweethearts. We didn't have much in common but we were the only two in the company who had grown up in Millersville, and it threw us together. We sat together on my dirty blanket in the near-dark, listening to the snores of some fellows and the laughter and swearing of others, and gobbling down the last of that tart pie. In between bites, I told him a little of what had happened that afternoon.

"Lordy be, Sol, you got yourself another sweetheart!"

"No!" I said, hard-like, and then lowered my voice. "No, it ain't like that."

"I don't know, Sol. I wished I had pulled her out of the river. I never have such luck."

He was so well intended I didn't mention the fact that he couldn't swim a lick, and even crossing little Paint Branch Creek near Millersville had turned him pale. "It wasn't all that lucky. I near on to drowned myself."

"But you met a girl," he argued, as if that single fact was enough to warrant drowning.

"Not much of a girl," I said consolingly, remembering Mahalia's cussing, and those trousers. But I didn't want to talk too much about Mahalia until I had a chance to figure her out, so I changed the subject. "How did drill go, anyway?"

"Hard. I'm so sore in the hind end I don't know if I can sit in a saddle tomorrow. Say, guess what we heard today?"

"What?"

"Lee's headed north with his army. His whole army."

"We've heard that before." We'd been camped near Washington D.C. the entire last winter, and every other week or so some fool Paul Revere shouted warnings that set folks to packing silver and building barricades in the streets.

"This time it sounds real."

"Well, good, then," I said, trying to sound soldierly.

"I don't know, Sol. They say the officers even are worried. Not about the Rebs, but—you know. About Colonel Miles."

We'd all heard the stories, about how Colonel Miles had been drunk while in command of a division at the first battle at Bull Run. Brought up before a military court, he'd sworn that the brandy had been prescribed by a doctor for medicinal purposes. He hadn't been discharged, but he was shipped from the front to command the garrison at Harpers Ferry. Colonel Miles was an old graybeard who should have been doing grander things. He'd been in the army since the Mexican War, but had never gotten higher than colonel. It worried some.

But I didn't want to talk about it. Maybe this sounds funny, but I didn't feel proper even thinking critical of my commanding officer, much less saying it. "I say let Lee come," I said instead. "We'll give him a run, now that we've got horses."

"You reckon so?"

I think one of the reasons I liked Randolph was that he was about the only one who acted less confident than I felt. "I surely do."

We settled down soon after that, and I was glad. Thoughts were whirling in my head like blades in a fanning mill. But before I could sort anything out, I heard Gillis's voice. "Hey, Hargreave! You going to be at saber drill tomorrow, or are you out to make some more of your pretty pictures?"

Sergeant Hailey stuck his head in the door. "Hey, shut up in there!"

Gillis let off, but he'd already spoiled the pride I'd felt that evening. My drawing had become a touchy spot. I like to draw, and I'm good at it. My mama always encouraged me, saying it was a "gentlemanly" skill. But it had gotten all mixed up in the ugliness that came after the war broke out. Most of the fellows signed right up and formed an infantry company. The cousins I'd grown up fishing with were first in line.

My mama begged me to stay home, and I was so used to doing what she wanted, since my pa died, that I agreed. But when all the parades and flag-presenting ceremonies and good-byes came, when folks were saying how good it was that local boys stuck by each other, a lot of meanness got directed my way. Most didn't say anything to my face, but I heard the talk: Poor Sol Hargreave, raised by all those women, no father to learn him, would rather sit and draw than fight when the country needs him. If he was a *man*—

Now, it seemed some of the boys in my regiment thought the same thing.

I had to remind myself that Colonel Davis had ordered me to do it. He liked the way I could draw a scene, quick and accurate—a mountain pass, a river ford, the lay of the land. We cavalrymen had to have that information.

Besides, I had other things to think about now. I was proud Colonel Davis had chosen me for another special job. But I was glad I had three days of hard drill between me and that job. I needed a plan, and just then, I had no idea what I was going to say when I presented myself back at Lock Thirty-Six.

CHAPTER FOUR

"Trust, gentlemen," Colonel Davis said. He was mounted on his huge gray gelding, and looked very commanding. "That is the key."

He had broken the regiment down by companies for morning drill. Company H was with him on a deserted stretch of Potomac shoreline. The morning was bright as a new penny, and when I looked across the river—toward Lock Thirty-Six, my mission for Friday—the sunlight dancing on the river hurt the eyes.

We'd arrived for drill looking good, I thought. We knew to show up for inspection with gleaming tack. Our government-issue cavalry uniforms were sharp. The foot-sloggers in the infantry wore all of a color, dark blue, with clumsy brogans and ridiculous hats. We had sky-blue trousers and dark blue shell jackets with the yellow trim that meant "mounted." And besides our sabers we had both Colt .44 pistols and Spencer carbine repeaters. I wished Betsy Lee could see me.

"You've learned the rudiments of drill," Colonel Davis drawled. "Now you need to go farther." Surprisingly, he smiled. "I want you to dismount. Remove your saddles and leave them on the rise. Oh—and leave your sabers too."

Colonel Benjamin F. Davis,
Eighth New York Cavalry, in
civilian clothes.

Civil War Library and Museum

Having gotten into the habit of regular drill, these orders made for some nervy looks among the ranks. Reluctantly, we piled our McClellan saddles in a forlorn heap behind us. With even more hesitation, our precious sabers were gently laid beside.

"Remount."

A couple of the boys turned back to get their saddles before realizing the colonel wanted us astride bareback.

I'm leggy, and in the confusion, managed to find a helpful rock and scramble astride. Some of the other fellows had a harder time. Poor Randolph never would have managed if Sergeant Hailey hadn't finally given him a boost.

We sat uneasy-like, waiting for whatever was coming next. "Gentlemen, you are coming to rely on the wrong things. You're trying to master your horses. You need to work *with* them instead. A good rider and good mount are one."

I thought he might say more, but a look at our gawking faces seemed to change his mind. "Gentlemen, form a line. Single file. I want you to canter to that fallen tree—" he pointed down the shore— "circle it, and return. Begin."

Captain de Vries didn't even try. He sat stiff in his saddle, watching, and Colonel Davis let him be. But the rest of us had to take our turn.

It sounds easy. But there were boulders on the route, a couple of gullies, all kinds of things to make the horses spook and start. Some of the fellows made it, but mostly by slowing to a walk on the tricky parts. Me, I'd woke stiff from my bangs in the river the day before, and slid off Cinder neat as butter halfway around the fallen tree.

I didn't feel good about that, but some of the fellows went off more than once. Randolph bounced along like a sack of flour, and fell three times. Gillis took a hard fall, and limped a mite when he took off after his horse, and I'm ashamed to say I took a bit of pleasure at the sight. Sergeant Hailey and Rusty, who'd grown up riding, were about the only ones to do it right.

Colonel Davis did not look impressed. "You're fighting your horses," he said, when we'd all taken our turn. "You need to trust them, and you need to let them trust you."

"I'd rather trust my saddle and saber," someone dared to say, loud enough to be heard.

A couple of fellows started to laugh, but choked it off quick. Colonel Davis glared. "And if your life depends on a quick escape?" he snapped. "You will take the time to saddle up? As for your beloved sabers—they make a fine display. They impress the ladies. And on a quick night bivouac, they work marvelously well for roasting meat over a campfire. But sabers are a poor defense against gunpowder."

His angry words gave me the spooks. I didn't like what he was telling us. Still, it was true that the Reb riders we were most likely to meet were known for hard riding, and more inclined to shoot from behind a tree than gallop up and politely request a mounted duel.

"Now. Try it again, and keep it at a canter. *Trust*, men. Trust your horses. Trust your own abilities—"

"Maybe it's having a Southern officer I don't trust," I heard Gillis mutter somewhere behind me.

"Yeah, and you don't see him trying it," Rusty muttered back.

I didn't think it was loud enough to be heard. But Colonel Davis, who had moved away, swung back with a hard look. He had heard, all right.

For a moment there was such a stillness all I could hear was some towhees calling up in the trees. I looked at the Colonel's face and felt something go cold inside of me.

Then he dismounted. "Hailey," he barked. "Remove my saddle." The sergeant jumped to obey. "*And* the bridle."

When it was done, Colonel Davis pulled aside the saddle blanket, as if even that was a nuisance. He put a hand on his gray's withers and murmured something. Then, with a swing so quick and graceful I hardly saw it, he was astride.

Colonel Benjamin F. Davis sat his horse like no one I ever saw. Without a word, without a visible move, the gray stepped into an easy canter. The Colonel rode with his hands held out from his sides—not for balance, I could tell, but to show he didn't need them.

We gawked in silence while they loped down the shore. Instead of circling the fallen tree, they jumped it. In that instant I knew what the Colonel had been talking about. It was like one creature soared over that trunk, as easy looking as a bird in flight.

When they circled back to join us he didn't look angry any more. "Are there any questions?" he asked. There were no questions. "Would anyone else like to ride without reins?" No one else wanted to ride without reins. "Now. Line up and try it again."

After evening mess Randolph and I wandered down Potomac Street. He wanted to find the regimental sutler, who usually kept his tent set up near one of the burned-out armory buildings. "I'm aiming to buy a pipe," Randolph told me.

"A pipe!" I didn't want to hurt his feelings, but Randolph didn't strike me as a pipe-smoking man.

"Colonel Davis smokes one," Randolph said, as if that explained everything. Which I guess it did.

The sutler was a weedy fellow. He wasn't official with the government, but followed us around. His prices were so high most of us didn't do much business with him. But the army was at times a bit on the paltry side with rations and such, so I guess he did all right.

Since it was harvest time he had a lot to offer that day, peaches and apples and grapes and a crock or two of marmalade he'd gotten off some farm woman. Randolph sniffed at a big twist of tobacco. My eye went to some lemon candy drops I particularly favor.

Another fellow was haggling with the sutler ahead of us. "But I don't have another dime. I'm good for it, though. I swear it."

"Sorry, lad, I don't do business on credit." He didn't look sorry.

"But I was up all night, coughing and sweating. We're supposed to get paid in two days. I'll throw in another nickel if you let me slide."

The sutler put the bottle of patent bitters he'd been holding back on the shelf. "No sale. Come back when you have the money."

The boy shuffled away, sneezing and muttering. I decided against the candy, and Randolph got disappointed too. "What you want a pipe for, boy?" the sutler asked, who didn't have any to sell. "All you need is a good plug to chew. I got the finest."

"I promised my mama I wouldn't chew," Randolph said calmly. The sutler turned away with a snort of disgust.

As we walked away a man in workman's clothing, who had overheard our exchange, gestured to us. "Say, boys, I have something you may be interested in." He rummaged in his pocket. With a look on his face that made me think he was about to extract a genuine jewel, he pulled out a couple strands of twine. "These here are pieces of the actual rope they used to hang old John Brown hisself. A real souvenir of Harpers Ferry."

Randolph, who had been dashed about the pipe, perked up. "How much?"

I elbowed him. "Didn't you already buy a piece? Back when we first got here?"

"Naw. That was a piece of wood from the scaffold. But this...."

The townsfolk, it seemed, had enough strands of genuine rope and splinters of genuine wood, all from the hanging of John Brown, to make a man think the scaffold was a mile high and just as wide. But Randolph had the right to spend his money how he saw fit, I figured, so I left him to it.

I had no mind to go back to quarters. I knew the boys would all be squabbling or cussing or gambling or trying to figure out Colonel Davis, and I didn't feel like taking part. Truth to tell, the only one I talked to much was Randolph.

I could have spent the evening writing a letter. I hadn't written my mama in a long time, and every letter I got from her scolded me about it. I'd sketched her a self-portrait of me in my uniform, and it was ready to send. It was hard to write her, though. She hadn't wanted me to sign up in the first place. And besides, I'd come to figure it was her trying so to change me, after my pa died, that had led to some of the hard things about my life. Fair or not, that's how I felt.

But I had my sketchpad with me. Drawing is good for occupying the mind without thinking. I wandered down to the Shenandoah riverbank and found a good flat rock near Herr's ruined flour mill. It had once made good use of the current, but had been destroyed the year before. Already weeds were growing up inside. It made an interesting picture, I thought, that ruined mill and the beautiful river. Since the evening was starting to wear I began quickly, so I didn't lose the light.

A couple of boys came by, with a good string of catfish. A bit later I became aware of several army officers walking along the shore, downstream from me. One was out in front, and he was peering across the river at Loudon Heights through field glasses. I wondered what he was looking at, but more than that, I tried to figure out what kind of hat he had on. He was in shadows, but I'd sure never seen the shape of anything like it. It was taller than a stovepipe hat, and lumpy.

A few minutes later a rider came up, picking his way among the rocks in the twilight. One of the men—not the one with field glasses—turned around real quick. "Who is it?"

"Private Higby, sir, looking for Colonel Miles. I was told he was here. I've been sent from Frederick."

The man with the funny hat put the field glasses away. "I'm Colonel Miles."

Colonel Dixon Miles, garrison commander at Harpers Ferry.
Harpers Ferry National Historical Park, National Park Service

Private Higby slid from his horse and saluted. "Captain Faithful sent me, sir. General Lee began bringing his army across the Potomac into Maryland this morning."

"Where?"

"The main fords near the Monocacy River. White's Ford, Noland's Ferry."

Noland's Ferry! That was only a dozen miles south of Harpers Ferry. I didn't think about how I shouldn't be listening, I'm ashamed to say. Instead I strained to hear more.

"What's their strength? Is this just a cavalry ploy?"

"I don't know, sir, but first indications were against it. Our scouts reported seeing what could only be the main body of the Confederate army. Captain Faithful didn't want to risk a wire. He said to tell you he'd send another courier as soon as he had more information."

Higby didn't know any more, and Colonel Miles sent him on his way. The Colonel and his aides seemed about to follow, but then he pulled out the field glasses for one last look at the darkening mountain ridge beyond the Shenandoah. "Thunderation!" he barked a moment later.

"There they are. Those cussed Rebels have the best signal system I've ever seen."

As they walked back toward town, I got a better look at Colonel Miles. He looked like somebody's grandfather. Then I saw something I could hardly believe. That funny hat wasn't a hat at all, but two hats. The man was wearing two hats, one right on top of the other.

When they had gone, I walked down the shore. I didn't need the field glasses to see what they'd been looking at. The twilight was about gone, and I could just see the black outline of the mountain ridge against a dark purple sky. But a light was showing from that ridge, blinking on and off unnatural-like.

It was a spooky feeling, I don't mind saying, watching communication going on, knowing it was the enemy, and not having the foggiest idea what was being said. I stood watching for some time, thinking about what I had heard, thinking about the Rebel lights, thinking about a garrison commander who wore two hats at once.

CHAPTER FIVE

A storm blew in that night, fierce enough to rip a few shingles off our quarters house. It also drove rain in through the window broken earlier in a rough indoor game of catchball, and the fellows in that corner whined about it all night. In the flashes of lightning I looked at my messmates' faces and thought they looked for all the world like scared boys wishing they were home.

I would have been awake all night even without the commotion. I couldn't stop thinking about what I'd overheard on the shore, picturing Robert Lee and his Rebels on the advance. I reckoned our own officers were probably in weighty conference with Colonel Miles, while the storm rumbled and flashed, figuring what was to be done. I reckoned we'd hear new orders in the morning—maybe to ride out to meet the Rebel force, even.

Those orders didn't come. In fact, nobody said anything about the Rebels crossing the river. Instead, we spent the next morning drilling in the muck. Colonel Davis was with another company, but Captain de Vries worked us hard enough himself. Whenever someone made him angry his face got red, and he smacked a little whip against his boot. That afternoon, we saw more boot smacking than ever before. "What's he sore about?" Randolph finally murmured to me, after another tirade, and I could only shake my head.

After being dismissed we had about an hour free before evening mess. I went back to quarters, hoping for a nap. I'd heard rumors that Company H was next in line for patrol duty, and I hadn't gotten much sleep the night before. Some of the boys took their clammy blankets down to the shore, hoping to dry them in the breeze, so it was fairly quiet.

But I'd only drifted off when Bushman, the private on duty downstairs, shook me awake. "Hargreave? There's some foot-slogger downstairs asking for you."

"For me?" I frowned. I couldn't imagine why an infantryman would be looking for me.

The fellow waiting impatiently in the street was a stranger. "You're wanted at the bridge," was all he said.

"The bridge? What for?"

"Provost guard wants to see you."

Bushman was following our exchange with interest. I decided not to ask any more questions. "Is Sergeant Hailey around?" I asked instead.

"Ain't seen him."

"Well, tell him where I went, will you?" I asked. Bushman shrugged.

Harpers Ferry was under martial law. The provost guard maintained a station at every access point into the town, including the Potomac bridge. I had passed through on Monday, with my pass from Colonel Davis, and could only guess that some question had come up about my trip to Maryland.

One picket was standing at attention on the bridge itself, rifle poised importantly across his chest. But my guide led me to the three-sided shed the guards used for shelter, or for detaining travelers without the proper pass. Inside I found two more soldiers—and Miss Mahalia Sutter.

She was wearing her ugly dress again, but if anything, looked less ladylike than before. Her arms were folded across her chest, and her mouth was pinched into a tight, angry line.

"Are you Solomon Hargreave, Eighth New York Cav?" one of the guards asked. He was a big, barrel-chested guy, with a funny nasal accent. Maine, maybe.

"Yes."

"This here *lady*—" he stressed the word, like it was some kind of joke, "asked for you."

"She did?"

"And she ain't got no pass!" the other guard exclaimed. He was a gangly boy with red hair and freckles.

"May I speak with Mr. Hargreave?" Mahalia asked the ground. Every word was clipped.

I reached for her arm, thinking to draw her away, but the big man knocked my hand away. "You two got talking to do, you do it here. She ain't got a pass to get in, and you ain't got a pass to get out."

I waited. Mahalia drew a deep breath. "I am real sorry to involve you, Private Hargreave. But it's true. I don't have a pass, and I can't ask for one unless I'm permitted to go on to the provost marshal's office. And these men will not let me go. And I have to get into town."

"What for?"

Her eyes found mine. "The baby—Thomas—he's sick. I need to get to the apothecary."

"These Maryland girls, they have all kinds of stories," the freckled boy cried. "We've heard about it. They warned us, didn't they, Will? They can't be trusted."

I have to admit, my mind was turning over the story Colonel Davis had told me the other night. Was Mahalia lying? Was she on some secret mission for her brother and his band of bushwhackers? I couldn't tell.

"I'm not looking to steal government information," Mahalia snapped, like she knew my thoughts. "And I'm not smuggling anything either, which I figure is also on your mind. I just want to go to the apothecary—"

"She probably doesn't even have a baby brother! She thinks she can smuggle medicine to the Rebs!" The young one pointed his gun.

"Hey, hold on!" Without thinking I put my hand up and pushed the gun barrel away. I wasn't sure of Mahalia's motives, but this redhead should never have been trusted with a weapon, that was sure. "She does too have a baby brother. I've seen him. I'll vouch for that."

"But will you vouch for her?" Will asked, with a smile I didn't like. "The only way I'll let her through is if you take responsibility."

Mahalia clenched her hands into fists. "Please, Private Hargreave." She couldn't even look me in the eye. She was not a girl to beg lightly, I knew. Either Thomas was truly sick or something else very important was going on.

"I'll accept responsibility," I said. My stomach suddenly felt like I was jumping off a cliff. What had Colonel Davis gotten me into?

The guard named Will made a big show of writing down my full name and unit, the time, and the situation. Then he wrote Mahalia a temporary pass: "To be used only for the bearer, Miss M. Sutter, to conduct herself from the Potomac provost station to the provost marshal's office," with the date and time and my name as escort all over again.

With the precious slip of paper in hand, Mahalia moved to leave. But as she passed by, Will put a big hand on her shoulder and ran it down her arm. "Come back any time, darlin'," he laughed. "Maybe I can convince you us Yanks ain't all so bad."

Mahalia wrenched away and marched off before I could even open my mouth in her defense. Since I was responsible for her, I had no choice but to follow. Judging by the size of Will, and the eager energy of his companion, I figured that was just as well. I didn't trust Will not to accost Mahalia, and I didn't trust the redhead not to shoot me in the back for letting my "charge" out of sight.

"I am real sorry," Mahalia muttered again, as I caught up with her. "But I just *had* to get into town, and I don't know anyone else in the military here. Yours was the only name I could think of."

"I'm sorry too," I said, grim. "I'm ashamed that Federal soldiers treated you so poorly. They're infantry. Not in my regiment."

She waved my embarrassment away. "I've seen the likes of such before. I'm worried about Thomas, not me."

"What happened?" I asked, as we headed for the provost marshal's office on Potomac Street. Mahalia was walking faster than any girl I'd ever seen.

"Thomas, he was up most of last night. Real fretful. Mama thought maybe it was a tooth coming in. But then he started wheezing. And coughing. I think it's the croupy cough. That can get real bad."

"Yes, it can," I agreed. I'd seen a neighbor's baby die of it, in Millersville.

"I went looking for the doctor in Sandy Hook. He wasn't in. But his wife told me he uses Ipecac on croupy cough. If I can just get some...."

A minute later she retold the story for the provost marshal, a tall man with bushy side-whiskers and an air of having heard too many sad stories, in his days at Harpers Ferry, to be much moved by them. "I'll give you until sundown," he said, and scribbled a pass. "You've got to be back in Maryland by dark."

Outside, I was surprised when Mahalia extended a hand—not to kiss, but to shake, man-style. "Well, thank you again, Mr. Hargreave. I'm sorry to have troubled you."

"Wait a minute!" I had to run to catch up with her. "I'm coming with you!"

"There's no need!"

"There is too!"

Her anger came back. "Crimus! Of course, I wasn't thinking. I'm your responsibility. You have to make sure I don't slip the ammunition I have hidden under my petticoat to Confederate sympathizers."

"That's not it," I sputtered, hoping she didn't notice the flush on my cheeks—or that if she did, she'd think it was only because I'd never heard a girl mention her undergarments before. "This town is no place for a young lady, is all. I'll see you safely back to the bridge."

Fortunately for my conscience, it wasn't even a lie. I hadn't forgotten Will's lewd remarks. And I hadn't been too lost in conversation to notice the hungry stares and whistles from soldiers we passed. I'm ashamed to say it about my own army, but there were thousands of soldiers in Harpers Ferry, a long way from home. The civilian population had dropped from three thousand before the war to only a hundred fifty or so, and young ladies were not prominent among them. My responsibilities aside, I was afraid of what might happen if I sent Mahalia on alone.

"Suit yourself. I don't have time to argue."

Mahalia seemed to know the way to the apothecary, and I figured she must have done business there before. But a cry of dismay escaped when we rounded a corner and found only the ruins of a frame house. "What happened to Mr. Billington's apothecary?"

"I guess he's gone," I said, which was stupid. A couple of foot-sloggers came out, carrying pieces of a broken table. "There's still plenty of firewood," one of them said generously, before balancing his booty on his head and trudging up the hill toward the encampment on Bolivar Heights.

"I was sure he'd still be here," Mahalia said. "The people— they need him. I was sure."

"Is there another apothecary in town?"

"No. There was one, before the war. But he left right away, before things even got bad." Mahalia took a deep breath. "I have to think."

"Maybe we can find an army doctor."

"An army doctor! They won't bother with a sick baby in Maryland."

"We can try," I said firmly. This time I led the way.

It took a long time to track one down. Military rules are so complicated. It's peeving at the best of times, enough to drive a man mad in a crisis.

We went first to the infirmary, and were met at the door by another guard. "Do you have a pass?" Mahalia offered hers. He squinted at it and slapped it back. "No, a pass to see a surgeon."

"Could I just talk to one for a minute?" I tried.

"Not without a pass from your commanding officer," the guard shrugged, and turned away.

I tracked down Sergeant Hailey next, who was glad to see me. "Tarnation, Hargreave, Bushman said—"

"It doesn't matter what Bushman said," I interrupted impatiently, aware of Mahalia's tense silence beside me. "My, uh, friend here needs to speak with a surgeon. Can you write me a pass?"

The sergeant shook his head. "Wish I could, but they won't take it from an enlisted man. You've got to go to Captain de Vries. I'll give you a pass to see him."

I hesitated. I'd hoped to avoid that. But Sergeant Hailey was a good fellow, and I knew he would have helped me if he could. "I guess that's my only choice."

"I'm running out of time," Mahalia said urgently, as I towed her along to Captain de Vries' quarters. The sun was sinking.

"I'll get you back in time." It was a reckless promise, but one I intended to keep. "And try not to worry about Thomas. I know your mama—"

"My mama and Phoebe," Mahalia interrupted in a flat voice, "will do their best. But they're not real good in an emergency."

Captain de Vries kept us waiting for ten minutes after the sentry had gone inside to find him. Mahalia stood hugging herself, her face closed with impatience and worry. I tried to think of how to best phrase my request.

"Sir, I was wondering if you would help us with a medical problem," didn't work. The Captain didn't even wait to hear me finish the sentence. "Who's this?" he barked, frowning down at Mahalia.

"I met her family on Monday when I was in Maryland, sir," I tried to explain. "Miss Sutter's baby brother is very ill. She needs to speak to one of the surgeons—"

"She must go to a civilian doctor," de Vries said. "Regulations. The military can't concern itself with civilian affairs."

"But sir, this is an emergency—"

He hadn't expected me to argue. Even in the fading light I could see the red slide up his cheeks, and his hand twitched as if longing for his whip. For a moment I forgot about Mahalia and wondered if I'd gone too far.

I heard the trotting hoofbeats, but didn't turn until they came to a stop behind me. "What's this?" Colonel Davis asked pleasantly. He and Major Corliss were evidently returning from an evening ride. "Good evening Captain de Vries, Private Hargreave. Is there some problem?"

"I was just explaining to Captain de Vries about this lady's emergency," I said quickly, before the Captain had a chance to speak. "This is Miss Sutter, Colonel. I met her family when I was in Maryland. Her brother is very ill, and the doctor in Sandy Hook was away, and the apothecary here is closed, and—."

"My sympathies, Miss," the Colonel said graciously. He gave no clue he'd ever heard the name "Sutter" before. "I'm sure one of the surgeons would be happy to give you some advice. Captain de Vries, do you have paper handy?"

Captain de Vries was standing like he was made of wood. After a pause he disappeared inside the house and returned with paper and pen and inkwell.

Colonel Davis held the paper against his saddle and scribbled. Then he handed the pen back to the Captain, waved the paper for a moment to dry the ink, and presented the pass to Mahalia. "Here you are, Miss Sutter. Ask for Surgeon Bicknell. He's a friend of mine."

"I thank you most kindly," Mahalia said earnestly.

"Colonel, do you think maybe I should see Miss Sutter home?" I asked. I didn't dare look at de Vries.

The colonel's gaze was calm. "Why, I think that's a fine idea, Private. Young ladies shouldn't be about unescorted at night. Don't you agree, Captain?" He held out his hand, and the captain handed him another piece of paper. Soon I had a pass as well.

"Thank you, sir." I saluted to the colonel, then the captain, before loping after Mahalia. I'd worry about Captain de Vries later.

"That man's Southern," Mahalia said.

"Oh—Colonel Davis. Yes, he's from Mississippi."

"He's your Colonel?"

"He surely is." I grinned. Miss Mahalia Sutter hadn't been expecting to meet a Mississippian in the Yankee garrison, that was certain.

"Interesting that the Southerner's the only polite one I've seen yet."

That stung. "How about me?" I demanded.

We'd reached the infirmary walk again, but she did stop and look me in the eye. "Yes. And you."

"And I'm from New York," I mumbled.

I don't think Mahalia heard me. She was already slapping her pass into the hand of the same guard who had denied us earlier. "We're here to see Surgeon Bicknell."

Surgeon Bicknell had graying hair and blue eyes that crinkled at the corners when he smiled kindly at Mahalia. Dark smudges under his eyes made me imagine long night hours spent tending the men in his care. "There, now Missie, don't fret," he told Mahalia. "I'll give you a couple grains of powdered squill. Mix it with a cup of hot boneset tea and try to get it down." We watched as he sprinkled the medicine on a slip of paper, rolled it up, and then tightly twisted the ends.

"Oh, thank you," Mahalia breathed. I could hear the relief in her voice.

"Give the lad a warm bath, too. If you've got mustard— have you? Got any mustard?"

"Uh, no sir."

"I'll fix you up with some." He rummaged among his bottles and pouches again. "Here. Apply a plaster to his feet. And put a steaming kettle in the room. Back home, I saw many an infant through bad spells of croupy cough that way. I know it's hard to go through it, but your brother's got a good chance of mending."

Mahalia fished in her pocket for a coin, but Surgeon Bicknell waved payment away. "The army's almost destroyed this town," he said sadly. "The civilian physicians have been driven away. It's a sorry day if we can't help a sick baby. You run along."

I didn't know if I should shake his hand or salute, so I did both. "Sir, I thank you most kindly," Mahalia said again. "I'm beholden to you."

"We have to hurry," I said when we stepped outside.

"There's no need for you to see me home," Mahalia said. "Good-bye."

"Why is it so hard for you to accept help?" I demanded. I wasn't about to let her face those provost guards alone again. I also knew Colonel Davis wanted me to go.

"Because I don't need help," she said, despite the fact that she wouldn't have gotten to see the surgeon without it. "Getting home, I mean," she amended, as if she realized how I'd take her words. "Look, I have to go now. It's almost dark. And I have to get home. They'll be worried."

"Colonel Davis wanted me to see you home. And it will be quicker on the mare." I turned toward the stable. She couldn't argue with that, and followed.

After saddling Cinder we rode back to the guard station at the bridge. I got some pleasure at Will's surprise when he saw us both heading to Maryland. We didn't even dismount, just handed down our passes for him to inspect. As we trotted away I thought I heard him yelp.

"What now?" I asked, wondering if I should stop.

"Keep going," Mahalia said over my shoulder. "I kicked him."

"You kicked the provost guard?"

"He pinched me."

I kept going. We took it slow across the bridge but once in Maryland I hit the towpath at a canter. When we reached the lockhouse Mahalia clattered straight upstairs. Without thinking I followed her.

Phoebe was sitting in one of the bedrooms with Thomas in her arms. Mrs. Sutter was hovering tearfully over her shoulder.

"Is he still alive?" Mahalia cried.

Phoebe didn't need to answer. Poor Thomas was wheezing and hissing for every breath.

"I've got some medicine. I'll go down and get it started." Mahalia pushed past me and ran back downstairs.

We found Clem in the kitchen, feeding the fire in the woodstove. Mahalia was all business. "Did the little ones get fed?"

"Yep. I sent them to bed."

"Good boy. Now haul me some water, will you?"

I helped Clem fill the buckets at the pump outside. Mahalia stoked up the fire and crowded the stovetop with kettles. Soon she had hot water for the tea and mustard plaster, and I carried up another bucket for Thomas's hot bath.

Mahalia gave Phoebe instructions before returning to the kitchen. Before I could lend a hand she swung a heavy iron kettle back to the stove. "I've got to keep water boiling, so we can keep getting some steam up to him."

"Wouldn't it be easier to bring the baby downstairs?" I asked.

She shook her head. "Too drafty. Now let's see. If I fill the coffeepot...."

Clem bit his lip. "Mahalia."

"What?"

"There's a tree got hit by lightning last night. A big branch split off and fell in the canal. I found it this afternoon."

"Did you get it?"

"Me and Howie tried, but we couldn't. I need you to come help me. If a boat should hit it—"

"I know." Mahalia bowed her head for a moment, her lips pressed in a tight line. Then she straightened up. "Go fetch Howie. He can listen for boathorns and watch the stove while you and I—"

I finally found my tongue. "Wait a minute! I'll help Clem."

She looked surprised, as if she had forgotten I was there. "There's no call—"

"Come on, Clem," I said.

I wasn't sure what I was offering my services for. But Clem knew what he was doing. He lit a lantern and slung a coil of rope over his bony little shoulder. "Come on. It's downstream about a mile."

The towpath was hushed. A barred owl called once, nearly spooking me out of my skin, but Clem didn't even twitch. He watched for landmarks I couldn't see. Even in the dark, he led me straight to the trouble spot. He held the lantern so I could see the blackened scar on a magnificent sycamore, and the huge limb splintered across the towpath and into the canal. "It's a sleeper," he said. "See? Most of it is just under the surface. A captain might not see it."

"Couldn't you have gotten help hauling this out? Someone from the company?"

"It's our responsibility," Clem said, uncoiling his rope. "Every lockkeeper is responsible for a section. Our piece is about two miles. I walk it every day. Come on." Without hesitation he splashed chest-deep into the canal.

I pulled off my boots and jacket before following him in. The water was cold, but at least it was still! "Every day?"

"Yep. It's in the contract. We have to maintain our lock, and the spillway, and our stretch of canal. Usually it's just filling holes in the towpath and such, but sometimes this happens. Wait. I'm going under."

He disappeared under the black surface. Just when I was about to panic he emerged. "Got it. It's knotted good.

Now I'm going to winch this around the trunk. When I holler, you push."

This skinny barefoot boy impressed me. When he hollered, I used every bit of strength I had, and Clem pulled with every ounce of his body too. It took a while, but we got that tree limb heaved safely up on the bank.

"Whew," I said, when the canal and towpath were clear. "I don't know that you and Mahalia could have gotten that out."

He dismissed that. "Oh, Mahalia's strong."

"Yes," I said, holding the lantern up so I could find my boots. "I'm learning that."

Back at the lockhouse we found Phoebe in the kitchen. The room smelled strongly of mustard. "How's Thomas?"

"Mahalia's sitting with him. I think his breathing is starting to ease a little. Clem, that kettle's coming to boil. Carry it upstairs, will you? And then you can change."

Clem reached to obey, but I grabbed the kettle first. "I'll get it. You go put on some dry clothes, Clem."

I went up real quiet, thinking maybe Mahalia had gotten Thomas to sleep. When I reached the doorway I saw Mahalia standing by the window. Thomas was in her arms. I could hear the baby's raspy breathing, but I could hear the quiet tones of a lullaby, too. "Hushabye, little one, sleep in peace when day is done—" She saw me and broke off.

I put the kettle down and came closer. "Is it eased some?"

"I think so. And I got Mama to lie down. Thanks for the water."

"I do think he sounds a bit better," I added hopefully. Real gentle, I touched the baby's cheek with my finger. It was soft, like the petals on a rose I'd once presented to Betsy Lee. I'd never touched a baby before. Mahalia didn't answer, just touched her lips to his forehead. I left them alone.

Phoebe was still in the kitchen. She looked strained, but still pretty, and she still found a smile for me. "You sit, Mr. Hargreave. You've done us a kind turn. I'm going to fix you a cup of hot tea, and get a blanket—"

"Oh, no thank you, Miss Sutter." It came out hasty and rude, but it was dark and late and I was uneasy with the notion of sitting alone with Phoebe Sutter. "If there's nothing else I can do for you, I have to get back."

"Oh, surely you have time to warm up! You'll catch your death. Please." For a moment a slim hand rested on my arm. "Look, you're shivering."

I couldn't tell her it wasn't just the wet clothes making me shiver. Lord, how she reminded me of Betsy Lee! "No thank you," I said, stumbling backwards to the door. "Please give Mahalia and your mama my regards—"

I hadn't counted on Clem. He burst out the door before I had a chance to mount. "Wait!" he cried, and darted to my side. "Mahalia said to give you her most kindly thanks. We're grateful for what you done."

Unexpectedly, I felt a ripple of guilt. My doubts about Mahalia at the bridge had been empty. She had been telling the truth about Thomas. Had Colonel Davis helped only because he thought she was a spy? I had come all the way home with her—was it just to see if her story was true? I didn't think so, but the question itself made me uncomfortable.

Clem was waiting. "It was nothing," I mumbled. With that I fled. If Colonel Davis was expecting information, he wasn't going to get any more than tales of a sick baby that night.

CHAPTER SIX

Company H was called for patrol on Friday. Some sniping was going on, and pickets were increased along the railroad tracks west of town.

I checked with Colonel Davis to see if he still wanted me to spend the day in Maryland. "About the other night, sir. I didn't get any information. Everyone was upset about the baby, and—"

"Hargreave, I expected nothing." Davis smiled. "You happened to be in a position to offer assistance. They got to know you a little better."

"So... you still want me to visit them again?"

"My orders stand, Hargreave. I still want to learn what we can about Corbin Sutter."

I considered asking what he knew about Lee's army. Word of the Rebel advance into Maryland hadn't gotten to the boys in my regiment yet. Did Colonel Davis know? The night I'd overheard Colonel Miles, I'd been tempted to go back to the house where Davis and Major Corliss were staying. "Private Hargreave to report, sir," I had imagined myself saying. "I came to make you aware of important reconnaissance information I just received from Captain Faithful in Frederick. General Lee has crossed the Potomac with his army, and is invading Maryland. His destination may be Harpers Ferry."

But I hadn't received reconnaissance information. I'd been eavesdropping. I figured I best stay silent.

It was an odd feeling to cross the Potomac into Maryland, alone and riding straight toward the Rebel army. Funny that I hadn't even thought about it when I was taking Mahalia home, so taken up with thoughts of the Sutters and their troubles. But today... I wouldn't have told a soul, even Randolph, but I was a mite jumpy. The entire Reb army was a considerable force. Besides, those local bushwhackers were no doubt feeling more bold with the news.

Then I looked at the high cliffs of Maryland Heights. Colonel Miles had ordered defense works to be built up there, and although some said they were shabby, it was a comfort to have Federal troops between me and the Confederate army. Besides, now that I was actually on my way back to the Sutter place, I had the prospect of seeing Mahalia to think about.

When I got to Lock Thirty-Six, Mahalia was in the garden digging potatoes. She was barefoot and in trousers again, her hair careless in an untidy braid down her back. After attacking a mound, she scrabbled through the dirt to find even the marble-sized spuds. I tied Cinder and watched for a moment from the corner of the house.

I wanted to make a sketch. I took a deep breath instead. "Good morning, Miss Sutter."

She was startled to see me, and didn't look pleased. Her greeting took away any doubt. "What are you doing here?"

"I came to talk to you."

"What about? I'm busy."

"So am I. But this is important."

Something in my voice must have convinced her. She wiped her hands on her pants. "Well, what?"

She sure didn't make things easy. But I had tormented myself too much about what to say, and how to say it, to back down now. "Three things. First, how is Thomas?"

"Oh." She blushed. "Better. He's better. We're grateful for it. And I'm grateful to you for helping Clem, too."

I didn't want any part of that gratitude. "I'm glad he's better. Now. The second thing. Miss Sutter, is your brother Corbin alive?"

She stared at me. "Do you know something about him?"

"No. That's why I'm asking."

"Well, I don't know. If he's dead, I mean." She was still staring at me, with narrowed eyes. "Why did you come here asking such a thing?"

"Because my Colonel, when I explained why I was late on Monday and he heard your name, asked me to find out."

"The colonel I met? The one who helped us?"

"Yes."

"Why? Why did he ask you that about Corbin?"

"Because it's his business to know. I mean, your brother was—is—riding at the head of the Loudon County Scouts—"

"So that's why you helped me! Dag bite it!"

"No, Mahalia! It's not like that. That's not why—"

The blare of a boathorn interrupted. Mahalia turned her back on me to go meet it. I was half-sorry and half-relieved.

I followed her around the house, and saw a coal barge sliding toward the upper sluice gate. It seemed only natural, since I'd done it the other day, to help her lock the boat through. She accepted without comment. But for the first time, we were doing something together, not fighting each other. It was like a silent truce had been called.

I didn't want to lose that feeling after we shut the lower gate again and waved the boatman on his way. "Look," I said quickly. "I admit I was surprised to see you at the bridge, and I didn't know at first what you were after. But I forgot about the war and everything, as soon as I realized how worried you were. About Thomas, I mean. I helped because I wanted to. And I didn't come here now to make trouble for you." I ran a hand through my hair, trying to figure out how to get through to this girl. "Can we sit down for a bit?"

So we sat right there, on the edge of the lock, with our feet dangling over the cut stones toward the water. Just then Clem, Howie, Rose, and Lizzie tumbled out of the house like puppies. That reminded me. "Clem!" I called. "I brought you some candy."

"Candy?" he echoed. He looked blank.

"Yes! My favorite kind." I rummaged in my jacket and pulled out a bag of lemon drops. I'd passed the sutler the evening before, and made the purchase. "You've got to share. You did such a good job the other night, I'm putting you in charge." I tried to look stern. "That's an order."

"Yes sir!" Pleased, Clem attempted a salute before accepting the bag. He hesitated when he opened it. "This is candy?"

"I got them each a peppermint stick last Christmas," Mahalia said. "That's what they remember."

"Well, this is good too. Try it!"

Cautiously, Clem put a piece in his mouth. In a moment he carefully doled out pieces to Howie and the girls. Soon the four towheads were sucking noisily. I felt embarrassed by their pleasure. Bringing them candy had seemed like a small thing.

"There was no call for you to bring them candy," Mahalia said. But she didn't look like she minded. She watched them finish, as if it was a treat just to see them enjoy themselves, before taking charge again. "Now, put the rest away for later," she instructed Clem. "Help them wash up at the pump, and then set the little ones to work on the pole beans. And watch them proper, now." They went without argument.

She turned back to me. "Why did you tell me that your Colonel asked you to come here?" Her voice was puzzled.

"Why? Because it's the truth."

"But you're asking questions about your enemy. You could have lied. Or at least been, oh, more roundabout."

"Yes, but... that wouldn't be right.

"It'd be easier."

"Well, maybe. But I wouldn't have felt right."

She picked up a pebble and tossed it into the canal, thinking. Finally she said slowly, "I've heard the talk that Corbin's dead. I've laid awake nights, wondering if it was true. But I've also heard talk that the Yankees made up that story—"

"The Yankees! Why would they—we—make something like that up?"

"Because my brother is a hero in these parts. They'd like folks to think he was dead."

I didn't like thinking that Yankees would make up stories. Funny, how each side thought the same way about the other.

"I don't know which story is true," Mahalia went on. "He used to come by when he could. We haven't seen him in three weeks. But I don't know if that means anything."

"Wouldn't someone have told you if he had been killed?"

Her face closed. "A body would think so. There was a time I would have sworn it. But Elisha, that is, Elisha Forbes, Corbin's best friend, who was riding with him, he hasn't been around here either. Not lately. He—" Her voice had been rising but she stopped, choking off whatever she was about to say. Then she looked at me and I saw her face was closed again. "You said you had three things to talk to me about. What was the last one?"

My face got warm. Truth to tell, as hard as asking about Corbin had been, I had more doubts about my next question. "Well, the honest truth is I wanted to make sure you were all right."

"I'm fine. Need more sleep, is all."

"I don't mean about staying up with Thomas. I mean about Monday."

"You saw me. I didn't come to no harm."

I tried again. "No, I don't mean about getting pulled out of the river," I made myself say. "I mean about... well, about you going in the river in the first place."

Mahalia stared down at her toes. For a long time I thought she wasn't going to answer. Then, "Forget about it."

"I can't!"

"It's not going to happen again." She gestured toward the house. "I have too much to do. They're depending on me."

"But they were depending on you last Monday, when you threw yourself in the Potomac!"

I could scarce believe I'd said those words. I hadn't planned to be so direct. Mahalia was not a girl who liked prying. I expected her to storm off.

But she didn't. For a long moment she looked away, and I couldn't guess what she was thinking. Finally she stared at her fingers and said, "Look. I'm not pretending things here aren't hard. I've got Mama to take care of, and the little ones... and I don't think a minute passes that I don't wonder if Corbin is dead or alive. Last Monday, well, something happened I hadn't expected. It just pushed me too far for a bit, and somehow I found myself out on that rock. I didn't even plan it. It just happened."

I wanted to ask what had happened on Monday, but didn't dare. "But... it worries me. What if you get more bad news—"

"It's not going to happen again," she said, real firm. "No matter what news I might get. I can take it. I have the family to look after."

"It's a mighty responsibility," I said slowly. I was thinking about Mahalia, but suddenly I was thinking about myself too. "I'm the youngest in my family, and my mama's always done fine taking care of herself. But I worry... I'm the only son. If I get killed she won't have protection when she's older, or any of my sisters who don't get married."

Mahalia nodded. "Our mamas take care of us when we're children. They need to know we'll take care of them when they get old."

"Mahalia..." it was the first time I'd used her first name, but she didn't seem to mind, "is your mama all right?"

Mahalia shrugged. "Mostly. She doesn't usually know that Pa Sutter's dead. Like I told you, he was the second husband that died on her. I don't want her to hear the stories about Corbin, either. She—"

"Why, Mr. Hargreave!" Phoebe came out the front door, looking as sweet and pretty as Mahalia did rough. She had on a nice dress, with one of those paisley-thing shawls around her shoulders, and carried a basket. "I didn't know you had come to call."

I scrambled to my feet. "Good morning, Miss Sutter," I said real quick. "I happened to see your sister in the garden, and I—"

"Oh, go on with your excuses," she said lightly, like I'd been flirting with her, in just the tone Betsy Lee used. "I don't have time to visit this morning in any case, I'm afraid." And to her sister, "I'm on my way to Granny Fosdick's. She was poorly yesterday, so I don't know when I'll be able to come home. I might even spend the night, if need be. With Thomas mending you can manage, can't you?"

"It's all right," Mahalia said. "I'll fix supper if you're not back."

"Are you on foot?" I frowned. "I could—"

Phoebe smiled. "Thank you, but I'm used to the walk. It's not two miles. Until we meet again—" She held out one hand for me to bow over. It was a pretty gesture, although I couldn't help noticing that her hand wasn't white and lily-soft as she probably would have liked. For a moment I felt sorry for Miss Phoebe Sutter as we watched her walk down the towpath. She wanted to be a fine lady, and life at Lock Thirty-Six didn't let her.

But then I looked back to Mahalia, and remembered who really carried most of the burden. "Is she of much use to you?" I asked, kind of abrupt-like, and felt my face go red again. "I mean—I didn't intend to be rude—"

"It's all right." Mahalia said. "Phoebe is... well, Phoebe. And actually she does help, in her way. She doesn't mind going to Granny's. Granny Fosdick needs someone. She can't take care of herself, but she's too ornery to give up her place and come live with us."

"Is she your mother's mother?"

"No, my pa's. My real pa. Mama had Corbin and Phoebe and me by my real pa, but he died when we were so small I don't remember him. Then she married again, and we switched our name from Fosdick to Sutter. I didn't mind. Pa Sutter, he was a good man. Granny Fosdick never liked him, though. She don't think so high of my mama either. That's partly why she doesn't want to come here."

I was surprised by this outpouring of conversation, but I didn't mind it. "Maybe she didn't like your mama getting married again."

Mahalia pulled up a piece of foxgrass and began tying the stem into little knots. "Well, my Granny Fosdick, she's a sharp old bird. I don't think she likes my mama because she isn't. Sharp, I mean. To hear her tell it, my real pa was the equal of five men. Able to do anything. Pa Sutter, he never was much of a success. He was a dreamer. We tried farming, but he lost the land. My ma loved him, though. I can say that."

"It's funny," I said, although it really wasn't funny at all, "I don't remember my father as well as I used to. Folks say he was a good farmer. They say he could sweet-talk the crops right out of the soil. I used to help him, trail along after him in the fields. I liked it. He used to say, 'Sol, this will all be yours one day.' He said that almost every day." It was the clearest memory I had left of him.

"So who's taking care of the farm, with you off to war?"

"We don't have it any more." I drummed my heels against the lock wall. "My mama, she thought she had married down. I don't think she liked being a farmer's wife. She sold the farm to my uncle after my pa died. We moved to town, and she kept me steered away from farming." And away from my cousins, which I hadn't understood at the time. How many times had she said it? The words still echoed in my brain: 'You are a gentleman, Solomon, nothing less.' And that soft, determined voice had pushed me toward studies, and drawing, and Betsy Lee Thornton.

"When Pa Sutter got the lockkeeper job, I thought we were going to be set," Mahalia said. "But then the war came.

He liked to talk fancy about the war. About ideals and causes and honor. He didn't have to go, not at his age. Got himself nothing but killed."

"It must have been hard on your family, even before that happened. I mean—your pa and your brother going in two different ways." I couldn't imagine it. Everybody in Millersville thought pretty much the same way about the war.

"It was hardest on Mama. She doted on Corbin, and on Pa Sutter too. But the two of them never really got along."

"Why did Corbin go South? Did he believe in slavery?" It was hard to understand how someone from a poor family would fight to defend slavery.

"Shoot. Slavery's got nothing to do with it. Corbin never talked about causes and honor, like Pa Sutter. Pa Sutter believed in the Union. Corbin mostly just likes a good time. He didn't like working the lock. He and Elisha had gotten jobs at the charcoal pits, but they didn't like that either. The war let them escape. It was an adventure. Lots of folks around here see Yankees as invaders, and the boys like to think about chasing 'em off. And we've got lots of Fosdick kin in Virginia."

I'm not sure how long we sat and talked. Looking back on it, I can see it was the first time I'd really talked to anybody in a long time. Randolph, he was a good fellow. But some people are like little streams. Randolph was like that, good and clear, so you could see right through to the bottom. I never got the sense that there was anything on Randolph's mind I didn't know about. Me, it seemed there was always a lot on my mind that no one ever knew. I was more like a river, too deep to see in very far. Mahalia was like that too. Truth to tell, I hadn't known how lonely I was. And Mahalia, I figured she was lonely too, even if she never would have admitted it.

Finally another canalboat interrupted us. I realized that too much time was slipping by, and that I better be on with my official business. I helped her lock the boat through, and though the last boat had helped us talk, this one seemed to remind us of other duties. "Look, I got to get back to work," Mahalia said, as the mules towed the boat away.

"Me too. But listen...." I didn't want her to get angry again, especially after having such a nice conversation. But I didn't want to worry about her, either. "Mahalia, I know you have a hard time here—" I gestured toward the house— "and if there's something I could do that would help, you got to tell me. If things with the family get too rough again—"

"It wasn't the family that got too rough." She wiped her hands on her trousers, looking down.

"Then what?"

She took a deep breath and looked me square in the eye. "Solomon, I've known lots of boys like you. I bet you got a real pretty sweetheart waiting for you back home. Have you ever been in love? Truly, I mean?"

That was like getting punched in the stomach. I finally gulped out a rough "Yes."

"Well, since you have, maybe you can think on what it feels like to find out the person you love, and trust, is secretly spending time with someone else. That's what happened to me. That's what sent me down to the river."

My head felt like it was about to explode. First, everything between me and Betsy Lee came rushing back like a train car. Second, and I don't mean this unkind, Mahalia Sutter, with her swearing and her trousers and her general bad temper, was not a person I would have imagined talking about such things. When she did talk about them, she used an odd tone. Not angry. Not weepy. Just telling the story, quiet-like.

"You ever been in the Salty Dog?" she asked.

The Salty Dog was a tavern along the canal near Sandy Hook. I don't know why it was called that, but I knew it was a favorite stop on this side of the river. "No."

"A girl sometimes works there. Her name is Lucy Torrison. She stopped by here the other morning to tell me she's getting married. To Elisha. The worst of it was hearing it from her. Elisha didn't even have the spine to come tell me himself. He and I—" Finally she stopped, her mouth clamped tight, like she was shutting a sluice gate over a flood of words.

"Why are you telling me all this?" I blurted out. I wanted to jump in the canal as soon as I'd said the words. The last thing I wanted to do was embarrass her.

But Mahalia wasn't embarrassed. "You were honest with me," she answered. "You didn't have to be, but you were. I figure I owe you the same. And, I don't want to give you cause to think any more about what happened the other day. It's done. It's behind. I'm grateful for your help with Thomas. But there's no cause for you to come back here again."

Well, there wasn't much more for me to say. If losing this Elisha hurt her anything like losing Betsy Lee hurt me, it was far from done and behind. But I knew better than to argue with Mahalia Sutter.

CHAPTER SEVEN

After leaving Mahalia to finish digging her potatoes I rode north, mapping some roads and making the sketches Colonel Davis wanted. When I got hungry, I bought a couple of apples from an old woman plucking a goose in her yard. "Hey Yankee!" she said with a toothy grin, after I'd tossed her the penny and was heading around to go. "You watch your blue tail! General Lee's across the river!"

That reminder didn't make me inclined to linger so far away. But I thought about the Colonel entrusting me, and I poked around good and proper before turning around. I came back along Harpers Ferry Road, winding beneath Maryland Heights and its comforting Union defenses, and felt better.

It was late afternoon by then. I could have crossed back to Harpers Ferry and met my company. But I couldn't stop thinking about Mahalia, and I had to just about pass the Salty Dog to get to the bridge anyway. Now, Colonel Davis hadn't said anything about stopping in a tavern. But the way I figured it, I'd already finished what he'd asked me to do. It wouldn't hurt a thing if I stopped for a bit. In fact, I reckoned perhaps I could pick up some important reconnaissance information.

Near the bridge to Harpers Ferry a few buildings huddled between a canal lock and Maryland Heights' towering cliffs. The tavern was a small frame room tacked to the side of Spence's stone store, with a bar along the back and a couple of tables. There were a dozen or so men inside, mostly locals, I guessed. I stood for a moment, looking around for a place to sit and suddenly feeling less comfortable with this idea. My mama was a charter member of the Millersville Women's Christian Temperance Union, and I'm none too familiar with the insides of taverns. There was no sign of a young woman, which meant this Lucy Torrison wasn't at work, and she was the one I'd been hoping to catch a look at. Besides, I noticed a few fellows looking at me funny, which made me jumpy, I'll admit. I was the only person in uniform in the place.

I was about to leave when a man called from behind the bar, "You want a drink, sonny?"

"No," I gulped. Then, because I didn't know what else to say, "I was just looking for someone."

"Who?"

"Lucy Torrison," I blurted. No other name was handy.

"She ain't working today."

I nodded and turned toward the door. But before I could leave, one of the drinkers at the corner table stood up. "Hey, what do you want with Lucy Torrison?"

I saw someone about my own age. He was dressed casual, in wool pants and vest with a dirty shirt. He had curly brown hair and wasn't as tall as me, but more stocky. I couldn't help noticing he had on high riding boots, though, and a pistol tucked in his pants. And that he looked angry. Suddenly it hit me hard that I was alone in a saloon full of men who, for all I knew, were inclined toward Rebel sympathies.

While I pondered that, the one who had spoke up took another step. "I said, what do you want with Lucy?" His hands clenched into fists.

Boat emerging from Lock 33 across the Potomac from Harpers Ferry. The stone building at right was Spence's Store, and the frame building attached to it is what is believed to have been the Salty Dog Saloon, where Solomon met Elisha in this story.

C & O Canal National Historical Park,
National Park Service

"Forbes!" It was the bartender. He hadn't moved, but his voice cracked like a whip. "I welcome your business. You know that. But I won't have trouble. You hear?"

This Forbes fellow looked like he would welcome some trouble.

I did something then I haven't told a soul to this day. "I'll just go," I mumbled to the bartender, and almost ran out the door. I flung myself on Cinder with a speed which would have done Colonel Davis proud, and kicked her into a quick canter.

No one followed. Before I'd even reached the riverbank I was cussing at myself. There was a bitter taste in my mouth. Here I'd had grand ideas of going back to Colonel Davis with reconnaissance information. Instead, any true tale would have to include running from a saloon brawl.

I had headed the mare toward the river, but I wasn't ready to cross that bridge back to Harpers Ferry. I was too ashamed to face Colonel Davis. And now that I was alone, I was ready to talk myself into making a stand. Let those fellows come! I'd be ready this time, and wouldn't turn tail like a rabbit.

But they didn't come.

Feeling low, I slid to the ground and wandered down to the river's edge. I pitched a few rocks into the current. Suddenly, while I was seeing everything in the saloon go by again in my mind, something else hit me.

The bartender had called the other fellow Forbes. Mahalia had said Elisha Forbes was Corbin's best friend. Elisha Forbes was the one who had broke her heart by getting engaged to Lucy. I'd been too worried about my own hide to catch on, back there, but now everything made sense. No wonder his ears had perked up when I mentioned Lucy, and he'd gotten so angry.

I'd blundered into a member of the Loudon County Scouts, and hadn't even known it! And I had flabbergasted him, no doubt, by showing up in my Yankee uniform looking for his fiance. It was almost enough to make me laugh. But the memory of stumbling out of there stung too hard.

I was staring across the river and trying to sort everything out when I heard someone call my name. For an instant I thought the Scouts had come looking for me after all. Then I recognized a familiar figure, fishing pole in hand, shambling my way. "Mr. Timmerman! Good afternoon."

The old man slapped his thigh, as if pleased with some joke. "I thought it was you. I thought, Now, if that isn't young Solomon Hargreave!"

"I see you're out fishing again."

"I fish these shores everyday, son. Not much else for an old man to do."

"You must live near here."

"Sandy Hook. Lived there all my life. What are you up to, this side of the river? Rescuing another maiden?"

"No sir. I was... ah, well, I just stopped at the Salty Dog."

"Thought you might have come over to see Mahalia."

I looked at him, wishing I knew more about him. Francis Timmerman was dressed shabbily, barefoot, with shoulder-length hair that hadn't seen a comb recently. But he was smiling in a way that let me know his mind was still in one piece, and he probably knew what was going on as well as anybody. "Well, truth to tell, sir, I did just that this morning. I wanted to be sure, um, she had recovered and all."

"Good for you, good for you. Mahalia Sutter, she could use some company."

"You know her fairly well?"

He chuckled. "What is it you want to know?"

My face got red. "Nothing in particular, really. I was just wondering... I've been hearing stories about her brother. Corbin. It's hard to know what to believe."

"Corbin Sutter? He's a wild one. But he's not the kind that means any harm. His mama never could handle him, even when he was small."

"It was probably hard, after her first husband died."

"Oh, that's the truth. Corbin was without a papa for a few years, and he was a terror. It's hard on a boy, without a father."

That observation made me feel worse. Being fatherless had turned Corbin Sutter wild? Folks said the same thing had made me tame.

Mr. Timmerman didn't notice my look. "The girls kept up with his pranks, for a while. Why, I remember one time Corbin dared Phoebe and Mahalia to a horseback race up Maryland Heights and back. Sweet Jesus!" He cackled with delight. "It was a fool thing to do. But nobody got hurt, and an old man can take some pleasure watching the young have fun—"

"Phoebe and Mahalia!" I had a hard time picturing Phoebe on horseback, or Mahalia having fun.

Mr. Timmerman nodded. "You got to remember, son, that was some years ago. Before Miss Phoebe growed into a proper young lady. Before times got so hard for that family, with the war and all, and Mr. Sutter going off."

I noticed that he didn't mention Mahalia growing into a proper young lady, but I could hardly argue with him about that. "And then Corbin formed up the Loudon County Scouts," I said, trying to steer the conversation the way I wanted it to go. "I've heard a lot of stories about the Scouts, but it's hard to find out anything for sure."

"Yes, I expect that's so."

"Like Corbin Sutter, for example. Some folks are saying he got killed."

"I've heard it. Couldn't tell you rightly or wrongly."

Well, it seemed clear I wasn't going to get anything worthwhile about Corbin from Mr. Timmerman. I decided to try something else. "Mr. Timmerman, do you know Elisha Forbes?"

"I know him. Mind if I go on, since you're of a mind to talk?" He gestured toward the water.

"No sir." I watched him bait his hook and fling it away with a gnarled but practiced hand. "I think I just saw Elisha Forbes at the Salty Dog."

"Could be, could be. He's a Maryland boy, knows these parts well."

It didn't seem right, somehow. Those bushwhackers didn't wear any uniform, so unless someone caught them in the actual act of making a raid or terrorizing someone, they could get away with going wherever they chose. I hadn't found out much about Corbin Sutter, but I was fast forming a particular dislike for Elisha Forbes. "I hear tell he's engaged to a girl named Lucy Torrison."

"Well, now, is that the truth? I hadn't heard it." Mr. Timmerman pulled his line in, clucked at the empty hook, and rummaged in his pocket for another worm.

"Do the Torrisons live nearby?" I asked. I wasn't sure if it was smart to be asking so many questions. But I didn't know how else to get the answers.

"They've got a hardscrabble place, up on Elk Ridge." He gestured toward Maryland Heights. "North of all that army commotion. They've got a little apple orchard. It's not hard to find."

I chewed my lip, considering. Elk Ridge was the long mountain crest running north from the cliffs of Maryland Heights proper. I'd been up that way earlier, scouting the trails for Colonel Davis. I thought I remembered the place, a little run-down farm with a small orchard beside the house.

I looked back at Mr. Timmerman. He was intent on his line, and didn't seem inclined to offer anything further. "Well, it was nice to see you again, Mr. Timmerman," I said politely. "I have to ride back to Harpers Ferry. I wish you a pleasant evening. Good fishing."

He waved his hand, and I swung back to the saddle. But before I could turn Cinder's head, I heard him speak again. "You know, Solomon, good fishing depends on a lot of things. Sure, you got to have the right bait. But sometimes what you need most is patience. If you got that, you usually catch what you want."

"I reckon so."

He nodded. "You look to me like you might have the making of one fine fisherman."

I opened my mouth to say something but he was giving me a funny look, and I got the sudden idea he wasn't talking about fishing at all. It gave me kind of a queer feeling, and I didn't do any more than nod good-bye.

I trotted the mare back toward the bridge, but pulled up in a grove of trees before reaching the sentry. My mind was whirling around like one of the Potomac eddies. What was Mr. Timmerman trying to tell me?

Elisha Forbes was in Maryland, right that minute. I knew that for a fact. I knew now where his intended lived as well. If Elisha Forbes was in Maryland, surely he would be heading up to see Lucy. If I could get there first—

But was that why Mr. Timmerman had told me so much? Did he want me to do just that? After all, what did I know about the old man? Maybe he was a Rebel sympathizer. Maybe he told me just enough so I would be fool enough to head up there, and get nothing but captured for my trouble. Maybe worse.

It was hard to know what to do. There were Federal troops bivouacked by Sandy Hook, and I could probably find some officer to send some Yankee soldiers to round up a known member of the Loudon County Scouts. But I was in no mood to go to strangers for help.

Part of me wanted to scoot right back to Harpers Ferry, report to Colonel Davis, see what he said. No one would blame me. No one would think less of me for that, even Gillis and Rusty.

But part of me was still burning with the shame of bolting out of the Salty Dog. That part of me had something to settle with Elisha Forbes. Maybe, if I was hid and waiting for him, and he headed up the mountain alone to see Lucy, I could capture him.

I pictured the scene, me riding into Harpers Ferry with my prisoner. 'Elisha Forbes, sir,' I'd say to Colonel Davis, real casual-like. 'He's with the Loudon County Scouts. I thought I'd better run him in.' And to Forbes, in a different tone, 'And you'd better tell the Colonel everything he wants to know.'

Randolph would be awed, and even Gillis would want to shake my hand. Colonel Davis would clap his hand on my shoulder and ask me to stop by his quarters, after he was finished interrogating the prisoner, so we could share a bottle of whiskey while I told my story.

Looking back on it now, it was a crazy thing to do. But I turned Cinder's head away from the bridge, and headed for Maryland Heights.

 C*HAPTER* E*IGHT*

Folks say Sandy Hook was named when a teamster and his horses got swallowed in a quicksand bed at the edge of the river. It was a tiny but busy village, with a row of houses facing the railroad tracks. The railroad company maintained a repair shop there, and had a station wedged between the tracks and the canal. There was another little store there too, and I thought about stopping, since it was nearing dinner time and I was getting hungry again. But I skirted around, not wanting to be seen. Unless he was mighty stupid, Elisha Forbes wasn't still sitting in the Salty Dog waiting for me to maybe return with a whole regiment of Yankees. And although there were Yankee troops nearby, there was no way of knowing how local civilians felt about things. I wasn't looking for trouble.

So I didn't go through Sandy Hook. Colonel Davis had given me the opportunity to look around before, and I had the lay of the land in my head. It wasn't long before I was south of the village. I passed the raw army road that led up to the summit, looking instead for an old rocky trail that had once provided the only access to Maryland Heights.

It wasn't the shortest route. The Harpers' Ferry armory works had once needed a steady supply of fuel, and charcoal makers had hacked a number of traces up to their huge slash sites on Elk Ridge. They cut oak and ash and hickory, and laid whopping circular piles of logs to tend and burn. But when the Rebels destroyed the armory, there was no more call for charcoal, and the fires went out.

Now their traces were already overgrown. So I avoided them, and the army road where I was likely to meet questions I couldn't answer. The old trail was steep but passable.

But I hadn't gone more than half a mile before I realized how stupid that was. If Elisha was heading up the mountain too, he'd be on this same path. And after giving him a good look at me in the tavern, I didn't want to meet up with him alone out here—unawares, I mean.

After sliding down I pulled the mare off the trail. I tried to lead her through the woods, but the underbrush was a tangle of sassafras and raspberry thickets, and it was slow going. Finally I tied her in a well-hidden thicket and went on alone. I took my pistol but, after considering, left the saber.

I don't know how long it took me to circle around to the Torrison place, but before I got there I was calling myself every kind of fool. Elk Ridge is rolling on top, but steep as the devil going up. Cavalry boots aren't made for that kind of climb, and the air being only mild, my wool uniform was more than I needed. My visions of capturing Elisha Forbes slipped away in a torment of sweat, mosquitoes, brambles, aching leg muscles, and burning lungs.

But finally, I crept up on the Torrison place. I edged around the yard and doubled back from the far side, through the orchard. A couple of stolen apples filled the hollow in my stomach, which helped my mood a little. I considered my options for getting closer to the house. Finally, I dropped down on my belly and crawled, trying best as I could to stay hid in the tall grass. There were lots of windfall apples rotting on the ground, which made a fine mess of my uniform.

Moving slow I snaked along, stopping behind a wooden platform holding a couple of coiled straw bee skeps. I was hidden from the cabin, I hoped, but close enough to hear voices through one of the open windows. The cabin was small, one story and a loft. There was a stable behind, and a bit of a garden, but it appeared to me like the Torrisons earned most of their living from their apples. And not too good a living, by the look of things.

As I lay there, looking the place over, I discovered something else about apple orchards. All those fallen, rotting apples attract a powerful lot of bees. When I was still they came buzzing around, going from one blob to the next, and making me edgy. Funny, in all the stories I'd heard about spies and reconnaissance work, I'd never heard of anyone plagued by bees.

Sure enough, I'd only been there a few minutes when I got stung on the cheek. Well, by that time I was ready to admit defeat. But just as I was about to wriggle back the way I came, a girl came out the front door. She was carrying a butter churn, and settled down on a stool in the front yard and went to work.

She was a big-boned girl, about my age, in a faded dress with hair as black as Mahalia's was yellow. I could only guess this was Lucy Torrison.

She had no cause to turn her head toward the orchard, and I was pretty well hid. But I didn't dare chance moving now. She churned up her butter, and washed it clean, but she didn't go back inside. I didn't move.

After a bit an older man came outside and settled by the door. "Nice evenin'," I heard him say, while he filled his pipe.

"Yes, Pa."

"You expecting the boys tonight?"

"Yes."

That seemed to be all they had to say to each other. They sat, Lucy staring off into the evening, her pa smoking his pipe. The bees kept buzzing, and I was starting to feel mighty cramped. But I didn't move.

An hour must have gone by before Lucy jumped to her feet. Being closer to the trail, she heard the hoofbeats before I did. But suddenly, half a dozen riders spilled into the yard.

Elisha Forbes was in the front, and I didn't even look at the others. Lucy didn't either. She ran to meet him, and when he flung himself to the ground, she threw her arms around him. "Elisha—"

He pushed her off. "We got to talk." He pulled her by the arm, kind of rough-like, I thought, closer to the orchard and away from the others.

"What's wrong?" she cried.

"Who's this Yankee fellow you're spending time with?"

I gasped out loud. Fortunately, Lucy did too, and covered up any noise I made. "What? What Yankee fellow?"

"Don't lie to me, girl."

"I'm not lyin'—"

"I saw him!"

"Saw *who*?"

She sounded bewildered, all right. It seemed to strike Elisha, because when he spoke again, his voice was lower. "Some puking Yankee came in the Salty Dog this afternoon, looking for you. Cavalry. Are you going to tell me you don't know him?"

"Elisha, I don't!"

"He asked for you by name, girl!"

Lucy grabbed his arm. "Elisha, I swear to you, I don't know who you're talking about. I swear it! I don't know why a Yankee asked for me. There's no cause for it. I swear it!"

"If you're selling us out to the Yankees, Lucy, I'll make you regret it. You understand me?"

At that Lucy got mad too. She drew back like he'd spit on her. "How can you say such an evil thing?" she hissed. "Didn't I hide you? Didn't I take care of you when you got hit last spring? Didn't I pass across the lines with bullets and powder hid under my skirt? Didn't I bury my only brother when the Yankees killed him?"

At that moment a bee stung my finger. I managed not to yelp but I did jerk my hand up, and it made a stir.

Elisha turned his head like a hawk. "What was that?"

"What?"

"I heard somethin'."

I shut my eyes, afraid to see him descend upon me. Lord almighty, if he found me he'd probably string me up twice over. Once for being a Yankee, and once for passing time with his intended!

Lucy came to my rescue. "Don't try to sidetrack me, Elisha Forbes. Just what is it you're doing, coming up here and talking to me like this? You've got no cause."

I opened my eyes again. Elisha was looking back down at her. I could tell he wasn't ready to believe her. Finally he said, "Lucy, you want me to marry you. I said I would. But now... how am I supposed to know if this baby you're carryin' is even mine?"

I gasped again with that revelation. But Lucy made enough noise for both of us. She pulled her hand back and smacked Elisha so hard across the cheek his head jerked. Then she burst into noisy sobs and ran away from him. She pushed through the others, who were still milling around the yard, and disappeared into the house.

Elisha watched her go before slowly joining the others. "What's the matter with Lucy?" Mr. Torrison asked him.

"That's what I'd like to know," Elisha growled.

That answer seemed to satisfy Lucy's father. "Hard to tell, with women," he said. "Well, her ma'll tend to her. "Have some cider, boy. You're behind."

A jug was passed to Elisha. He took a long swig. "Whoo!" he said appreciatively, wiping his mouth.

Mr. Torrison laughed and slapped him on the shoulder. "My first run of the year. It'll be better in a week or two, but it's got a kick, even now."

Lucy seemed to be forgotten. As the riders relaxed with their jug, I took a good look at the others. And suddenly, I saw him.

He was on the far side of the group, dressed in the same rough, easy clothes. A shapeless felt hat sat low on his forehead. But not so low I couldn't catch glimpse of hair yellow as cornsilk. And when he turned his head, and I saw him in profile, I saw the same nose I'd seen before.

Now, the light was starting to fade, and it's true that I hardly had a clear view. But as I peered at him, I knew. I simply *knew*. He looked just like Mahalia, just like Phoebe. Without a doubt, I was looking at Corbin Sutter.

"Where you boys headed?" Mr. Torrison asked. "You got trouble planned?"

It was Corbin who answered the question now, like the leader he was, although his voice was so low I could hardly hear. I strained to catch what he said, sure I was going to get some important enemy information. But, "Not tonight. Ben's got a couple of turkeys hanging back toward the creek. We're going to drop them by the widow Patterson's place in Brunswick."

After all the wild tales I had heard about the Loudon County Scouts, the biggest plan they had for the night was delivering turkeys to a widow? I was supposed to report that to Colonel Davis?

Mr. Torrison, though, didn't seem surprised. "Where's the rest of the boys?"

"Scattered," Elisha said. "We're laying low for a couple of days. We're going to meet up at Zeke Cherry's place Monday night and hit the railroad on Tuesday morning. A friend of ours in Harpers Ferry said it might be worth our while."

Mr. Torrison knocked the dottle from his pipe and began filling it again. "I thought you might be thinking about heading east. Joining up with the regular army, now they're just a stone's throw away."

"Shoot! As long as there're Yankees in these parts, we figure to stay around."

Talk turned away from the war after that. They passed the jug around again, and the talk got louder and rowdier. Then somebody said something about mounting up.

Listening to them, I'd stopped being scared for my own hide. But it never pays to forget danger when you're in a perilous situation. While the boys were getting set to leave, Elisha turned and walked straight toward me, into the orchard. I could only think he was coming to investigate the sound he'd heard before.

The twilight shadows had stretched out by then, and it was gloomy in the orchard. I was scrunched behind the platform, and tried to press myself into the earth. Every muscle locked tight. My heart was thumping so loud I was afraid Elisha could hear it. My mouth went dry. I even found myself praying silently: *Please* don't let him see me. *Please* don't let him see me.

I couldn't look, with my face pressed into the grass, but I heard his footsteps stop a few yards away. There was another sound it took me a moment to recognize. My nose caught something besides dirt and apple. Elisha hadn't come into the orchard to find a skulking Yankee. He'd come to relieve himself. I was so thankful I almost did the same thing.

The Scouts rode off whooping and hollering. Lucy came out at the last minute to see them go. Elisha hung back for a minute, but I couldn't hear what he said to her. Then he ran and vaulted into his saddle from the back, something I had heard tell of but never seen done, before kicking his horse off to catch up with the others. I couldn't help swallowing some grudging respect. Anybody who would hit that trail at that speed in the dark was either a complete fool or one wondrous fine rider. I suspected it was the latter.

I remembered how I had tried to impress Mahalia by hitting the flat towpath at a canter in broad daylight, and was mortified. My new skills didn't stand up against these mountain folks. They knew the land and had been riding wild all their lives.

But at that moment, it didn't matter. It didn't matter that I had run from a fight in the Salty Dog, or that I hadn't captured Elisha Forbes. It didn't matter that it would take me hours to pick my way down the mountain in the dark and get back to Harpers Ferry. It didn't matter that I'd been scratched by brambles and stung by bees, or that my uniform was caked with apple slime and I'd come close to getting peed on as well.

What did matter was that I had some honest-to-God reconnaissance information to give Colonel Davis. Corbin Sutter was alive, and planning to hit the railroad Tuesday morning. And I was the only one who knew it.

CHAPTER NINE

I reported to Colonel Davis at two-thirty in the morning. The late hour and my mucky uniform added to my accomplishment, I reckoned.

The aide who spoke to me first looked sleepy. When Colonel Davis appeared a few minutes later he was pert as ever, in full uniform except for the jacket. I wondered if the man ever slept.

I made the story short, trying to keep my voice as cool as I had always imagined I would. When I told him about the train, Colonel Davis smiled. It was a long, satisfied smile. I was glad he had chosen to fight for the Union.

"Good work, Hargreave," he said, drumming his fingers on the table. "So they're planning to hit the train Tuesday morning, eh? Seems to me we might be able to do something about that."

"Yes sir."

"Jenson!" The aide appeared. "Go wake Corliss. And bring me the railroad timetable, here to Charles Town. And the map of Loudon County." Jenson quickly complied.

The Colonel, it seemed, was going to make his plans then and there. For a moment I thought he'd already forgotten me. He reached for a bottle of whiskey and poured himself a glass. Suddenly, he looked up at me and grinned. "You a drinking man, Hargreave?"

Should I tell him I'd never tasted whiskey in my life? Should I say yes, and have him think I spent my time at saloons? "Uh, only on special occasions, sir," I finally stammered.

Colonel Davis splashed half an inch of whiskey into a clean glass. "Here. You earned it."

It went down my throat like flames. But I took it in one gulp, and didn't even mind that the Colonel's mouth twitched toward a smile. "Thank you, sir."

"You're dismissed, Hargreave. Go get some sleep."

"Sir?" I hesitated, not wanting to ruin the moment. "I was wondering... do you suppose it would be all right for me to tell Miss Sutter her brother is still alive? Nothing more. Just that."

He regarded me. "Has the family invited you to return?"

"Actually, no." I didn't mention that Mahalia had made it plain that she didn't expect to see me again. "But I just thought she, that is, the family, has a right to know."

"I see no harm in that. Talk to Captain de Vries about it."

My face got hot. "Well, sir, it might be better if you gave me the pass."

"I see. Yes." He scribbled a pass for Sunday afternoon. "I'll send a message to Captain de Vries."

"Thank you, sir." I started to salute, but a final question popped out. "Uh, Colonel? I was wondering about something else too. Would you have let me help Miss Sutter the other night if you hadn't known about her brother? If you hadn't known anything about her at all?"

"Yes, Hargreave. I would have. No young lady should be about this town without an escort. And no young lady should be denied medical assistance for a sick child."

A wave of relief swept over me. I hadn't known until that moment how much it mattered.

It didn't take long for the story about Mahalia appealing to me for help to wiggle through the company. As a topic of conversation, it ranked with discussion of Lee's plans for his northern invasion. Most of the fellows hadn't had a girl to talk to in a long time. Some just wanted to ask me about it, wishing they had such a story to tell. Others enjoyed tormenting me. "So Hargreave, how's your Reb sweetheart?" Gillis asked every time he saw me.

Even Captain de Vries had a comment. "Hargreave must have his mind on a certain young lady," he said one day for the whole company to hear, when I made a mistake during drill.

"Never mind," Randolph counseled that night. "It'll pass. I heard today that Lee and the Confederates are in Frederick. Once that gets around—"

"Where did you hear that?"

"In the bakery. I stopped after drill, and a courier came in. He'd just come from there. Anyway, once that news spreads, they'll all have other things to talk about."

They certainly would. Frederick! Hardly more than a stone's throw from Harpers Ferry. At that minute, I almost wished Lee would hurry and provide some distraction.

Because of all the jesting pointed my way, I was less reluctant to ride out of Harpers Ferry the next afternoon. Lee may have been in Frederick, but there were still two mountain ridges between us. At the moment, that was good enough for me.

At the lockhouse, laundry was dancing on the line and Clem was skinning a muskrat on the front steps. He smiled when he saw me, and wiped the blade of his knife on his pants. "Hey, Solomon!"

"You fixin' dinner?" I asked, hoping I wouldn't be invited to stay.

"I trap 'em for the company. They pay for the hides of beaver and muskrat because they do so much damage."

I saw Clem eyeing my jacket pocket. He was too mannered to ask. But when Rose and Lizzie came around the house and saw me, they had no hesitation. "Did you bring candy?" Rose asked. She was a sweet little towhead, with dusty bare feet and hopeful eyes. Lizzie, who was three, hung behind, regarding me with a thumb firmly planted in her mouth.

"Maybe," I said, and made a big show of searching all my pockets before finding the little sack. I'd brought licorice twists, so they had something new to try.

Mrs. Sutter heard their squeals and came to the lockhouse door. She looked more tired than the last time I saw her, I thought, but she smiled. "Why, Mr. Hargreave! How kind of you to call. Do come in. My husband was sorry he missed you when you were here. Perhaps you can meet him today. He should be home soon. Mahalia's in the kitchen. I'll fetch her."

Mahalia looked only mildly put out to see me, and didn't ask me what in tarnation I was doing there. That was a good sign, although perhaps it was only due to her mama hovering around. Instead she said, "Solomon? Why are you here?"

"Mahalia!" Mrs. Sutter clucked. "Ask Mr. Hargreave to sit down. Perhaps he would like something to eat."

"I don't want anything," I began, but at the same time Mahalia said, "Ma, I got that tea made for Phoebe. You best take it up while it's hot." Her voice came out louder than mine, and she caught her mama's attention.

"I'm sorry," Mrs. Sutter apologized to me. "But my daughter Phoebe is ailing, and I—" Thomas's unhappy wail fell down the stairs and cut her off. She sighed. "Excuse me."

"How's Thomas?" I asked Mahalia.

"Much better."

"Good. Mahalia, I need to talk to you. Can you come outside?"

"Not right now. I've got things to take care of."

Mahalia looked tired, too. She headed back to the kitchen and I followed her. "What's the matter with Phoebe?"

"She's been getting these spells, lately. She just needs to rest. I told her to stay upstairs. I don't want the little ones catching something." Mahalia was packing some cold ham and biscuits into a basket. "I've got to go up to my Granny Fosdick's. She was expecting Phoebe again today."

"Who's going to take care of the lock?"

"Clem and Howie can manage. Clem's already walked the level today, so he can stay put."

Rose and Lizzie pattered into the kitchen. "Mahaly, Sol brought us more candy!" Rose announced.

"That's lovely," she said, and to me, "You shouldn't spoil them." But she didn't seem to mind.

I watched while she wetted a cloth and gently wiped two sticky faces clean. "I have to go to Granny's now," she told them. "Phoebe's upstairs, and I want Mama to rest too. Will you mind Clem while I'm gone? I told him to give you bread and jam later, all right? And Rose, can you finish shelling those beans?"

"Yes," she said to all of it. "Come on, Lizzie." She towed her sister out the back door.

I didn't want to talk to Mahalia about Corbin in the house, just in case her mother came back down. "Well, when you're ready, I'll walk with you a bit."

After Mahalia got everything tucked in her basket, she called up the stairs to let her mother know she was leaving. Mrs. Sutter came back down. "Oh, Mr. Hargreave, you didn't even get a proper visit."

She looked so disappointed I pressed her hand. "I'm going to escort Miss Mahalia to her grandmother's, ma'am," I said, and she brightened up.

"There's no call for you to do that," Mahalia said, when the door closed behind us.

I took Cinder's bridle so I could lead her as we walked. "I don't mind," I said, and it was true. "Anyway, I've got something to talk to you about."

"I thought we did all our talking Friday morning."

"Mahalia, Corbin's alive."

That stopped her, all right. She stared at me. "How do you know?"

"I saw him."

"Where?"

I took a deep breath. "Well, I was up by the Torrison place on Friday night. I can't tell you all the details. But I'm sure I saw him. He looks just like you and Phoebe, right?"

"Right," she murmured, sounding funny. "Folks always said we looked like peas in a pod."

"I knew it! Anyway, I wanted you to know. As of Friday night, at least, he was alive and well."

She closed her eyes for a moment, and took a deep breath. Then she opened them and began walking again. "That leaves another question. Why hasn't he come by the house to let us know he was all right? Mama's been looking and looking for him."

"Well, I can't answer that," I said uncomfortably.

"What was he doing up at Torrisons'?"

That, too, was tricky ground. "Just visiting, it looked like to me."

"Was he by himself?"

"No, there was five or six others." And to save her from asking, I blurted out, "Elisha was one of them."

"How do you know Elisha?"

"He, uh... somebody called him by name. I heard it."

"I see." Mahalia walked ahead, real brisk. "Well, it's no business of mine."

I didn't know if I should say any more or not. I mean, I didn't want to hurt her by bringing up sorry details. But then, I didn't like holding a secret from her either. Military details—those I could keep to myself. But this was personal, and strange as our meetings had been, we'd always been honest with each other. "Mahalia."

"What?"

"Look, I don't know if I'm right in telling you this, but...." I took a deep breath. "I found out something else Friday night. The reason Elisha and Lucy are getting married is... she's going to have a baby." I couldn't even look at her, I was so mortified to say such a thing to a girl. My face felt like it was on fire.

But Mahalia didn't blink. "I suspicioned as much."

"You what?"

"Well, something had to make him propose to her so quick! I'm not a fool."

No, that Mahalia Sutter was not. "Well," I managed finally, "maybe it will make it easier for you, knowing he was, you know, that sort. And Lucy, too."

"That sort?" She threw me a look. "What do you mean by that?"

"Mahalia—"

"What sort?"

"You know what I mean." It was hard to believe I was having that conversation.

"You said you had a sweetheart at home. Do you mean to tell me you never done it?"

I felt like she'd slapped me. That she dare say such a thing about me, and about Betsy Lee! Betsy Lee Thornton, who was everything sweet and good, who had never done more than give me her hand to kiss and once, the night we were betrothed, her cheek. "I certainly have not!" I flared. "I wouldn't do such a thing."

She pressed her lips together. "It's not so horrible," she said quietly, and walked up ahead of me.

I stared after her. So she and Elisha.... And that she would admit it! A couple of wood ducks flew up beside me, barking their protests at our intrusion, and I scarcely noticed.

Then I felt the anger drain away like water out of a lock. She hadn't meant any harm, I could tell. And although everything about my upbringing spoke against what she had done, I knew she wasn't an evil person. I couldn't even think of her as a bad person.

"Mahalia, wait!" I called after her. And when I had caught up, "I'm sorry. I didn't mean to hurt your feelings."

"I didn't mean to hurt yours," she answered, quiet-like, and we both put that minute of ugliness behind us. "I guess I just figured... well, I figured anybody leaving for the war like you done would want to, if you were truly in love."

"It wasn't a matter of wanting. It—it's forbidden. But for another thing, by the time I left for the war, I didn't have a sweetheart any more."

"Oh." She thought on that for a moment. "What happened?"

What happened? Truth to tell, what happened was something I had never talked about to anyone, even Randolph. But suddenly, amazingly, the words spilled out. "We were engaged to be married. Everything was perfect. But then the war came. My mama didn't want me to go. So when all the other boys were forming an infantry company, I didn't sign up. And one evening, while we were sitting in her parlor, she told me she couldn't marry a coward. I said I would sign up after all, if she wanted, but she said it was too late. She didn't want to marry someone who would only serve his country to earn a woman's love. She gave me her ring back." I swallowed hard, and tried to keep the bitterness out of my voice. "And before the company even left for training, she was engaged again. To a lieutenant."

Somewhere during that speech we had stopped walking, and Mahalia put a hand on my arm. "Solomon, I'm sorry," she said simply. "I can tell you loved her real well."

"Yes, I did," was all I could manage. But I was grateful for her gesture. In a strange way, I felt a little better for telling the story.

"I loved Elisha very much too. That's why I let him have his way with me. We used to go back to this little grove in the woods, and it was like—like an island, in the middle of all the trouble. I'd never really fit in with anybody before. I never had anybody I could count on. It was the first time in a long time I felt happy. I thought we were going to get married. I thought he was going to help me with—with everything, back at the lock. I wouldn't have done it if I didn't love him."

"I know that."

"And trusted him. I believed the things he told me."

"I believed the things Betsy Lee told me, too."

For a moment we stood looking at each other. Then Mahalia asked, "How long has it been since this Betsy Lee did that?"

"Oh... a year and a half."

"Do you still think about her every minute?"

I knew exactly what she meant. "Not quite. But maybe... every hour."

"Does it get any easier?"

I thought that over. "At first, my heart felt like... like somebody was squeezing it with a handful of broken glass. Now... now it feels sort of like a cold stone."

It sounded stupid, but she nodded. "I think I'm still in the broken glass part."

We walked on in silence for a while. But it was a companionable silence.

"My turn-off is up ahead," Mahalia said. "You can turn back if you want."

"I'll take you all the way," I protested. Suddenly I laughed out loud. "We're not thinking, either one of us. Why are we walking when we've got this fine United States cavalry mount? Come on, I'll ride you to your grandmother's." I swung into the saddle and held her basket while she came up behind.

"You must think I'm a poor horseman," I said suddenly.

"Why?"

"Mr. Timmerman told me about you. He told me about a certain race—"

"Oh, shoot. He told you about that race up to Maryland Heights?"

"Yep."

"That was Corbin's idea. Folks still talk about it." Her voice was a mix of pride and embarrassment.

"I envy you. We only had draft horses on our farm, for the fieldwork, and a Morgan trained to harness for the buggy. I never rode. I'm trying to make up for it now, but it's hard." We'd come to the junction. A narrow bridge crossed the canal to the road, and beyond I could see a steep trail winding up the mountain. "Is this where I turn?"

"I could show you a couple of things."

"What?"

Mahalia slid down. "I could show you a couple of things, if you want. About riding."

"Really?" I considered that. I could almost hear Gillis and Rusty screeching, From a *girl*? But what would Colonel Davis say? I figured he'd take help from any quarter offered. I wasn't too proud to do the same. "All right." I dismounted too.

Mahalia ran an appreciative hand over Cinder's withers. "Did you choose her?"

"No. The army chose for me."

"You were lucky." Mahalia slipped knowing fingers along the bridle bit, peering. "She's got a good mouth. She hasn't been abused. Here. Let's take the saddle off."

I groaned. "Not you too! The Colonel would like you. He wants us all to be able to ride bareback."

"It's good practice. A saddle can get in the way, especially when you're just getting to know a horse."

The first thing she showed me was how to swing astride. She was as graceful as the Colonel had been. "Now you try. No, don't push up like that. You're using your arms too much. That won't work. Jump at the same time you swing your leg. Let your leg carry you over."

It took me several times but finally I scrambled astride, the first time I'd ever done so without a boost. "I did it!" I crowed, feeling like a kid who just learned to tie his own shoe.

She had me practice riding bareback. "Go straight from a walk to a canter - no!" I had nudged Cinder only to a bone-jarring trot. "Go back to a walk and try it again. Get used to skipping the trot. You hardly ever need it."

The towpath was a good place to practice, flat and almost deserted. Before long I was able to canter away, turn, and canter back without falling.

"Good!" Mahalia approved.

"It felt good," I said. "But I should probably get you to your grandmother's."

"Wait. There's one more thing I want you to try. Let me show you."

I watched while she vaulted astride. She leaned down and murmured to Cinder. Then she carefully brought her feet beneath her and raised first to a crouch, then a full stand on the animal's back.

"Mahalia, don't. You'll fall!"

"No I won't." She positioned her feet carefully, wriggling her toes, and clucked to Cinder. My mare stepped out in an easy, rocking canter. My jaw dropped. Cinder had never cantered for me without leg pressure.

Mahalia rode Cinder out of sight around a bend. I waited a full five minutes before they appeared again. Mahalia looked pleased with herself as she dropped to the ground.

"I'm not trying that," I informed her.

She tossed her braid over her shoulder. There was a look in her eye I'd never seen before. "I know. It was wicked to say you ought to. I was just having fun." She busied herself with the saddle blanket. "Come on. I better get going."

"I'm not sure even Colonel Davis can do that," I marveled, adjusting the saddle. "Lordy be, Mahalia!"

"It's not that hard, once you get your balance. Try it barefoot sometime, so you can feel her muscles."

"Where'd you learn that?"

"Corbin taught me. Corbin can do anything on a horse. He can mount a running horse as it goes by. We had some good times, before the war."

Mahalia's grandmother lived in a tiny cabin halfway up the ridge. The trail was as tortured as the path to the Torrison place. "You can see why someone needs to look in on her," Mahalia said. "It isn't good she's up here on her own, but she won't come down. Ride without stirrups for the rest of the way. It'll be good practice."

When we reached the clearing I dismounted too. "I'll come inside with you, just to make sure everything's all right."

"No, don't!" Mahalia said forcefully. Then, kind of sheepish, she added, "I mean, it isn't a good idea. Granny, well, she has certain ideas—"

"I'll just come in for a minute," I said, real firm. I didn't like the idea of leaving Mahalia in this isolated spot.

Mahalia hesitated a moment more and then shrugged and led me to the cabin. "Granny?" she called, pushing the door open slowly. "Granny, how are you?"

"Phoebe?" The voice that answered was stronger than I'd expected. "Phoebe, is that you?"

The cabin was one room, and dim. As my eyes adjusted I made out a cold hearth and a few pieces of furniture. The room smelled stale.

"No, Granny, it's me, Mahalia." Mahalia went to the bed in the corner, where a tiny old woman was propped against some pillows.

"Where's Phoebe?"

"She's ailing today, Granny. She—"

"I want Phoebe!"

"She's sick herself, Granny. So I came to see how you're feeling today."

I was hovering in the background, but I caught Mrs. Fosdick's eye. "Who's that with you?"

"Just someone who gave me a ride—"

"Come over here." And to my surprise, she grasped a stout stick leaning against the bed and pounded the floor with it. "Come over here!"

I answered the summons, but as I started to introduce myself, she interrupted. "God almighty, you fool girl, you come with a dad-burned Yankee?"

Mahalia threw me an 'I-told-you-so' look before trying to soothe her grandma. "Granny, he just—"

"What's your name, boy?"

"Solomon Hargreave, ma'am."

"Where are you from?"

"New York."

"Well, we don't like Yankees around here. If you had a lick of sense you'd go back to New York."

She was every bit as cranky as Mahalia had said, that was sure. I didn't know what to say, but Mahalia spoke up instead. "Not everyone feels that way," she said, quiet and firm. "My pa, for one—"

"Your pa is dead and in the ground, and I do not mean that fool Sutter," the old woman snapped. "Your pa was a real man. He wouldn't stand for such if he was alive. He'd be ashamed of you. How can you be Corbin's sister? Corbin is making his daddy's memory proud."

My mama had taught me to respect my elders. But I couldn't listen to that, and I didn't want Mahalia to be scolded anymore either. "Now just a minute, Mrs. Fosdick," I said. "Mahalia is taking care of the family. I think that would have made her daddy proud too, if he was the man you say."

The eyes in her dried-persimmon face glittered. "Well, at least you've got a bit of spine. For a Yankee."

I considered that a victory. "Good day, Mrs. Fosdick," I said in my most pleasant voice. "Mahalia." I gave Mahalia a look of apology before backing out the door.

As I left, I heard Mahalia say something to her grandmother about supper, which was ignored. "I want Phoebe!" Mrs. Fosdick said, and I kept going.

I decided to wait for Mahalia out by the trail, though. I was in no hurry, and I thought it would be nice to give her a ride back. I didn't mind sitting there, feeling the sun on my face, hearing a couple of blue jays squabble every bit as noisy as old Mrs. Fosdick. Looking back on it, I remember feeling peaceful inside. It wasn't a feeling I had often.

I waited only about an hour before Mahalia appeared, swinging her empty basket. She looked surprised to see me, but not unhappy. "You could have gone on."

"I know. But I wanted to apologize for getting you in trouble with your grandmother."

"Oh, don't mind that. If you hadn't come in I would have gotten scolded for something else. I don't know how Phoebe bears it."

It seemed natural to ride back down the valley with her behind. I took her all the way back to the lockhouse. "I thank you for the ride," Mahalia said, sounding like she meant it. "Well, I better go in and see how Mama's making out."

"Mahalia, wait." I kind of blurted that out, and after she stopped I tried to figure out what it was I wanted to say. "Mahalia, I... I never met anyone like you."

"I never met anyone like you before either, Solomon."

"I guess I just want to say... well, thank you. Not just about the riding. For talking to me, I mean. And for listening. You could shock the worms out of the ground, sometimes, but still... I'm grateful for it."

"Well, I thank you too," she said, looking me straight in the eye in a way Betsy Lee would never have done. "I get a funny feeling about you, Solomon. I get the feeling when we talk like you're telling me the truth. It makes me think on how little I've heard it."

Remembering Betsy Lee, I knew just how she felt.

"Solomon?"

"Yes?"

"Are you going to go after Corbin? Is your regiment, I mean?"

"We'd have to catch him first," I said, meaning it to be a joke, but she didn't smile. "Mahalia, I don't know what's going to happen. My colonel didn't say much about it. That's all I can tell you."

She accepted that, but something else was on her mind. "I've never understood why men go off to war. They all seem to have their own reasons, including you. I don't know that I've heard a good one yet. Do you like being in the cavalry?"

I considered. "Well... it's not what I thought it would be. I mean, it all seemed real clear back in New York. It hasn't been that at all. First, not having horses for so long, then getting a Southern colonel—well, not what we expected. And coming here, the Maryland border, where everything's so mixed up...." I shrugged. "I'm not sorry I joined up. But like I said, not what I expected."

"What are you going to do when the war's over?"

"Go back to New York State, I guess. But then... I don't know. My father wanted me to be a farmer. My mama wanted me to be an artist. Betsy Lee wanted me to work in her father's store—"

"But what do _you_ want to do?"

I gawked at her. Funny as it sounds, no one had ever stopped to ask me that before. I didn't even have an answer.

Then the sound of a child's wail drifted out of the house. That caught her attention, but before letting her go in, I stopped her again. "Listen, there's something else. What with the Rebel army moving in Maryland, anything could happen."

"What do you know?"

"Nothing, really. Lots of rumors are floating around Harpers Ferry. Some people still say they're headed this way. Other folks are saying it's Pennsylvania, or Washington, or New York City. But there're two armies moving as close as Frederick, and everyone's skittery. There's really no telling what could be coming. And my regiment could get called to move on at any time, without notice."

"I reckon so."

"Just be careful. All right?"

"Yes, I will. I better go in now."

I wanted to tell her I hoped I would see her again. I wanted to tell her not to work too hard, too. I wanted to say, Take time to ride bareback, and get that laughing look in your eyes again.

But knowing she was going into the house to check on her poor mama, and ailing Phoebe, and her younger brothers and sisters, and that she had a lock and a garden to tend as well, it seemed a foolish thing to say.

CHAPTER TEN

The next morning, while the rest of the company saddled for drill, Randolph and I trotted out of Harpers Ferry. "This was fine of you, Sol," Randolph said earnestly, for about the hundredth time. "Mighty fine."

"Aw, hush up," I said, mostly because I didn't want him to keep going on about things. But his happiness pleasured me. Randolph asked for so little in life. It was fun to suddenly give him something more than he'd ever expected.

This particular expedition had come about because of another meeting with Colonel Davis, who'd sent for me after I'd gotten back from visiting Mahalia. "Are you up to another assignment, Hargreave?"

"Yes sir!"

"According to what you told me the other evening, the Loudon County Scouts are planning to rendezvous at a Zeke Cherry's place tomorrow night, with plans to hit the railroad the next morning. I've done some checking. Their friend was well informed. There's a shipment of arms and ammunition passing through Tuesday morning that the Confederacy no doubt badly wants and needs. I'd like to keep the Scouts from getting their hands on it."

"You want to ambush them?" I blurted out.

He smiled, tolerant-like. "Before I can do that, I need to know their strength. We have our regular patrol duties, and with the Reb army just over the mountains, we don't have the luxury of extra men. I want to set up a surprise for the Scouts, when the train moves out, but I can't spare a single man more than I have to. That's why it's important to know their strength. Right now I don't know if I'm facing ten riders or forty."

I nodded, trying to look more experienced than I felt.

"I tracked down this Zeke Cherry. He's a well-known Reb sympathizer. He runs an inn about halfway between here and Charles Town. It sounds like the right spot for what they have in mind, fairly secluded. It's down by the river, far enough from the railroad to avoid the regular Federal patrols, but close enough to base a quick raid. I need someone to get set someplace in the vicinity early tomorrow morning, before any of them are about, to lie in wait and ascertain their strength. Then, we should still have enough time to mobilize before the train pulls through. You've been in on this from the beginning, Hargreave. Do you want the assignment?"

"Yes sir!" It wasn't the ambush I'd had in mind. But I had a funny feeling about that anyway, seeing it was Mahalia's brother, and I was still prouder than a new papa to have the colonel call on me like this. I'd deal with the reality of skirmishing with Corbin Sutter when the time came.

"Take someone with you. I'll release you both from general duty tomorrow. Who do you want?" He scrabbled in his little lap desk for a pass.

I didn't even think about it. "Private Randolph McCallister."

He looked up. "McCallister? You might want to reconsider. There are better riders in the company. Better marksmen too."

"Yes sir, there are. But Private McCallister is the one I trust."

He gave me a long look and then reached for the inkwell. "Private McCallister it will be."

That's why Randolph and I were on our way, heading southwest on a gray misty day. We'd been down this general direction a few times before, because Colonel Miles's "Railroad Brigade" had been patrolling the stretch of Winchester and Potomac line tracks between Harpers Ferry and Charles Town for weeks, and Company H of the Eighth New York Regiment had taken its turn. But today was different. We weren't on routine patrol. Randolph and I had a mission, an honest-to-God order for reconnaissance from Colonel Davis himself.

We didn't have any trouble finding Zeke Cherry's inn. It was a rough-looking place about ten miles out of Harpers Ferry, tucked up a little ravine above the main road that runs along the Shenandoah River. To me, it looked more like a tavern than a proper inn—the kind of place frequented most by those wanting nothing more than a drink, with a crowded room or two available upstairs if the drinking got too heavy, or the weather turned bad.

Randolph and I left the road and carefully edged around. I was feeling experienced, after my trek up Maryland Heights to the Torrison place, and Randolph cooperated by amiably following my every direction. The slope was steep and craggy, and he was puffing before we'd gotten very far. But truth to tell, only a bit harder than me.

We found the perfect lookout, a flat slab of rock on the ridge above the tavern. After picketing the horses in a handy spot and bellying out on the ledge, we peered over and considered. We were too far to hear anything, but we had a clear view of the inn and the road. Each of us had field glasses, and with those, I didn't doubt we'd be able to do all the counting we needed.

"What do we do now?" Randolph asked.

"We wait." I was propped on my elbows, scanning the top and behind of Cherry's place, looking for I don't know what.

"Sol?"

"Hunh?"

"Once we know how many are riding with the Scouts, do you suppose Colonel Davis'll send us to ambush them? Or does he have to report to Colonel Miles? I bet Colonel Miles would send those Illinois boys. They've got more experience."

"I don't know what will happen. Colonel Davis didn't say too much."

"Oh." There was a long pause, and then, "Sol?"

"Hunh?"

"How would you feel about it? Getting sent on the ambush?"

I put down the glasses and looked at him. "Do you mean, would I be scared?"

He looked startled. "No, I mean, you know, about fighting Corbin Sutter. Knowin' his sister and all. What if you killed him?"

I almost wished Randolph had asked about being scared. It wasn't something the fellows ever mentioned to each other, but I wouldn't have minded talking it over with him. I wondered if Randolph, who took life so easy, didn't even worry about such things. As for fighting Mahalia's brother, well, like I said before, I had no answer for that. "I think we'd try to capture them."

"Yes, but what if he was about to shoot, and you had to shoot first?"

"I'd shoot, I guess." I didn't add that I'd far rather take aim at Elisha Forbes. In addition to shaming me at the Salty Dog, there was the whole issue of his mistreating Mahalia. And Lucy too, come to think of it. I didn't care for that fellow, and if I ever got the opportunity, I was going to even that score.

"I guess you'd have to shoot him," Randolph agreed solemnly. "But I sure would hate to see that, Sol. I was hoping maybe this Mahalia would help you get over Betsy Lee. I know you said you weren't sweet on her, but you keep going back over there—"

"I'm still not sweet on her," I said. "But... I like her. I guess we're friends." It was the first time I'd thought of it in those terms. I'd never had a girl for a friend before. It was funny. But it was nice.

Well, me and Randolph had a long, miserable day. Once we'd found our lookout spot, there wasn't anything to do. That would have been trial enough, but the sky never cleared, and from time to time a cold rain drizzled down. We hadn't thought to bring our gum blankets. For a while we took turns, one person keeping watch while the other huddled under a big old oak tree, trying to stay dry. But soon we were both wet to the skin. I shivered and shook and wondered at the turn of events that found me, Solomon Hargreave, lying on a rock in the rain in Secesh Virginia.

By suppertime, when the rain finally let up and the sun was at least skirmishing with the black clouds for skyspace, I was dreaming about hot coffee. Some hardtack and water from our canteens didn't do much to either warm us up or fill our bellies. I didn't say anything, though, because Randolph never complained, even though he was probably even hungrier than me. I was glad I had picked him for company.

"Here comes two more." Randolph was peering through his field glasses. "No... they're passing on by. That's only three that's gone inside so far. Say Sol, how are we supposed to keep count? What if some of them inside are just plain customers?"

"I think we count everyone who goes in. If someone comes out and rides away, we take him off the list. That train doesn't go through 'till early tomorrow, so unless they have other business tonight, they'll probably be staying put." I didn't say it, but I reckoned I'd rather give Colonel Davis a number too high than too low.

Randolph nudged my arm. "Hey Sol. Take a look."

I grabbed my field glasses and followed his pointing finger. Six... seven... eight riders appeared on the road from the south. I focused in on them. One or two looked familiar, I thought, and they all looked like bushwhackers, well armed and dressed for hard riding. They were laughing and looking real at ease. I frowned, trying to get a look at the others... and then I saw Corbin. He was riding on the outside of the group, away from me, so he'd been blocked for a moment.

But it was him, all right. The sky was clearing, and I had better light than I'd had the other evening at the Torrisons'. Even though he had on the same slouch hat, pulled down low, I could see him plain.

"That's him," I hissed to Randolph. "On the far side, riding the roan. That's Corbin. And beside him, in the red shirt... that's Elisha Forbes. I don't know the rest. But down there, Randolph, are definitely members of the Loudon County Scouts." Randolph whistled appreciatively.

My field glasses were trained on the Scouts while they trotted up to the inn. I was feeling good, relieved things had worked out. Corbin and Elisha had actually turned up here, and in the daylight so I could see them for sure. I'd been a mite concerned that everyone would arrive in pitch dark. Then Randolph and I wouldn't have known what to report. If I had been a bushwhacker, I would have taken more caution. Even though we were in Virginia, it was close to the border, and Federal troops were stationed only a few miles away.

Well, it was a lesson they learned the hard way. What happened next came so fast and unexpected that later I had a hard time describing it to Colonel Davis.

Half a dozen Yankee cavalry came pounding up the road from the other direction, shooting and hollering. That put some life into the Scouts, I can say. About half of them had dismounted, and they scrambled mightily to get back in the saddle. I saw one of them swing up and then slide right over the other side, shot. He landed in a heap.

I thought the rest were going to run but instead they clashed right there in the road. It was hard to see what was going on, Yankees and Rebels all mixed up, the horses plunging and rearing. I saw the glint of one or two sabers but Colonel Davis was right, even up close those fellows were relying more on their pistols than their blades. We could hear the shots and all the yelling.

One rider broke away, headed south. I was surprised to see it was Corbin. The Yankees saw him too, and more than one must have took aim. The beautiful roan stumbled, fell on its knees. I knew it had been shot. Corbin lost his saddle. He hit the road hard.

Then I saw the flash of a red shirt. Elisha had seen Corbin go down too, and was coming to help. He leaned low from his saddle, one arm outstretched. Corbin grabbed it and swung up behind his friend.

But as he did, his felt hat flew off. A long braid of yellow hair flopped down from underneath.

They pounded furiously down the road and disappeared from view, with Corbin hanging on tight. Only it wasn't Corbin. It was Mahalia.

CHAPTER ELEVEN

Neither Randolph nor I said one solitary word on the ride back to Harpers Ferry.

We arrived in the early evening, when most folks were starting to ease down for the day. Randolph called greetings to a couple fellows from our regiment lounging outside the bakery on Shenandoah Street, but I barely noticed. At the corner of High Street I reined the mare to a halt.

Randolph went on a few steps before turning around. "Come on. We got to report to Colonel Davis."

I shook my head. "I don't know what to say."

"You got to tell him the truth, Sol."

So Randolph had seen her too. It had happened so fast, in the middle of everything else, I hadn't been sure. In a way, I was glad he'd seen. Otherwise I might have been tempted to lie.

We found Colonel Davis and Major Corliss eating supper, but their plates were almost lost in a litter of maps and papers. A sketch or two of mine was among them, but any pride I had felt about them was gone. I didn't feel like a soldier, like a cavalryman, any more. As Randolph and I saluted, I saw us as I figured the officers saw us: two boys, children really, one tall and skinny and one a little on the pudgy side. And the tall skinny one, at least, was feeling as low as a slug belly.

I let Randolph do most of the talking. But when he got to the part about Elisha's escape, I made myself tell what I had seen. Every word ripped at my insides. "The way I figure it, sir, Corbin Sutter must be dead after all. Ma—his sister must be riding in his place."

"I thought you said she was confined to the lock?"

"That's mostly during the day. And the boys can manage if they have to. Like you said before, Colonel, Corbin Sutter was a leader and a local hero. To keep morale up, and keep folks at least guessing, all she had to do was slip away every now and again and let people get a look at her." I'd had the ride back to town to figure it out. It all fit.

"It's a damn shame the two of them got away," Major Corliss said.

"I regret we were too far away to do anything, sir," I said, staring at my boots. It was the right thing to say. I didn't know if it was true.

"I don't believe any of them got captured, sir." Randolph picked up the story. "It all happened really fast. Both sides were about matched even, but after all the shooting commenced, some fellows ran out of the inn, and that overbalanced the Yankees. They lit out back the way they came. But a couple of the Scouts got wounded, or maybe even killed. We couldn't tell from where we were."

"Well, there's the end of our plan for tomorrow morning." Colonel Davis drummed his fingers on the table. "Foiled by our own side. I'll talk to a few people. I'd like to know who intervened so handily. Thank you, Private Hargreave, Private McAllister. You're dismissed."

We heard later that the Yankees we saw were from Cole's Cavalry, local Maryland boys who'd had more than one run-in with the Loudon County Scouts and had a score or two of their own to settle. They'd happened on the bushwhackers by chance, that afternoon, and seized the opportunity. Known casualties among the Rebels: two dead or wounded. Among the Federals: one mortally wounded. And one trompled heart.

I took Mahalia's betrayal powerfully hard. I went over every conversation in my mind a million times. I couldn't get it out of my head. It all circled around, buzzing like an angry bee in Torrison's orchard. I didn't hate her for being a Rebel. I could respect a person's choice, even if I didn't agree. But Mahalia had lied to me. I hated her for that.

And I hated myself for being fool enough to swallow it. Hadn't I seen her in trousers? Hadn't I seen her handle Cinder like the best bushwhacker in the county? Hadn't I seen enough of these border folks to know that it was never easy to know their allegiances? Why had I been so quick to believe she wasn't a Rebel when Corbin, her own flesh and blood, was a leader of the Loudon County Scouts? Nothing in that house had made good sense. I should have been more cautious. I thought of a dozen possible clues I had missed. And when I brooded over my last conversation with Mr. Timmerman, I came to wonder if he had been trying to give me a hint. I thought about it all until my head ached.

I can't say it hurt as bad as when Betsy Lee Thornton broke off our engagement and just as quickly got engaged to someone else. After all, Mahalia had never pretended to be a lady, and I had not been in love with her. But I'd been duped by a woman once before, and should have been wiser. Instead, I had trusted her, even told her personal secrets. Things no one else had heard.

The knowledge that I'd let myself get tricked again, that I couldn't trust even my own judgement, was bitter. But the situation confounded me. Was her devotion to Corbin, to the Confederacy, so strong that she was able to put aside her heartache and ride beside Elisha? To see him with Lucy, up at the Torrisons'? Or was everything she told me about her and Elisha a tale too?

I spent that evening down by the riverbank, sometimes staring across the rapids to the Maryland shore, sometimes making sketches of Mahalia and Betsy Lee like a man tormented. (Once I drew them holding hands, laughing.) The next day I rode through drill like I was asleep. It's a good thing we didn't get hit by any Rebels when we went out on patrol that afternoon, because I sure wasn't alert and fit.

The next two days were more of the same, and I finally figured I wasn't going to have any peace unless I crossed the Potomac again and confronted Mahalia. Anger was beginning to mingle with the hurt, which I guess was a good thing.

I wanted a pass to go back to Maryland. I couldn't go to Colonel Davis on my own, but I was desperate enough to consider Captain de Vries.

Sergeant Hailey looked doubtful when I talked to him about permission to see the captain. "Uh, I'm not sure that's a good idea, Hargreave."

"I know he doesn't like me. But I have to try."

"Sure you do, boy. Good luck with it."

The sergeant probably thought I wanted to keep a tryst. I didn't tell him the truth, and I didn't tell Captain de Vries either. The captain was about as helpful as I'd expected. "Why are you asking me for a pass to Maryland? You haven't been acting like a member of my company for the past two weeks, why start now? You have business in Maryland, you talk to Colonel Davis."

Well, it was better than a straight denial. I took his sarcasm for permission to approach the Colonel.

"He's not here," Jenson told me when I knocked at Colonel Davis's quarters on High Street. Then he peered at me in the fading light. "Oh. You're the one who did the drawings for him?"

"Yes sir."

"Well, I guess it's all right. He and the Major are in the stable."

That surprised me. I had figured officers left stable chores to privates. But I went around the house to the little back lot.

I heard the two men talking before I saw them. "...just don't understand it. Downey swears to seventy thousand, as close as Boonsboro." That was Colonel Davis's voice.

Major Corliss answered. "And Miles still believes they're only scattered."

"Foragers, Miles said. Foragers! I tell you, Augustus, I have a bad feeling."

I had stopped in my tracks, holding my breath to hear more, but about then I realized I better make myself known. I coughed and said, "Colonel Davis?"

I could tell I had startled the two of them. Major Corliss was sitting on a gear crate, twiddling an unlit cigar in his fingers. My colonel was currying his beloved gray.

"Private Hargreave," he greeted me, when I presented myself with a stiff salute.

"Forgive me for interrupting, sir. Captain de Vries sent me. I hoped for a word with you. The aide told me you were here. I came to ask permission to go back across the Potomac tomorrow. Any time that's handy. It won't take long."

"What is the reason for your request?"

"I, well... I have business there, sir."

He regarded me for a minute, and I thought I saw some sympathy in his eyes. But, "I'm sorry, Hargreave. Permission denied." Before I could respond, he said, "All the wires in and out of Harpers Ferry have been cut."

I had been so tangled in my own misery for the past couple of days I had plum forgot about the Rebel army moving in Maryland. But that night, whispering to Randolph what I had been told, and overheard, it all came back to me that something mighty serious was going on.

"All the wires cut." Randolph chewed on that for a minute. "That's bad, Sol. That means no one knows for sure what's going on over there."

"That means the Rebels don't want us to know what's going on over there," I clarified. "I don't know who this Downey fellow they mentioned is. Probably some scout, I guess. But it sounded to me like Colonel Davis thinks some of the Rebs are maybe heading this way."

We found out the next day that Colonel Davis had been right. A Confederate force had moved to Pleasant Valley, on the other side of Elk Ridge in Maryland. All that day the rumors flew around Harpers Ferry like swallows in spring. We privates sometimes felt we were the last to know anything for certain. But if the officers weren't saying much, the townsfolk, who always seemed to have their own information, said plenty. All day we saw them, the few who were left, trundling west out of town with handcarts and wheelbarrows loaded with quilts and food and silver candlesticks. They'd been through this before. Randolph and I tried to stop one to get the news. "You poor sots," he said, but wouldn't linger and talk.

That was a Friday. By evening we heard the first rumbles of gunfire on Maryland Heights. It faded off again, as twilight smoothed over the hills. But there wasn't a one of us in Harpers Ferry who slept good that night. I tossed on my blanket in torment, wondering both about the artillery on the cliffs, and the occupants in the lockhouse beneath it. Was Mahalia out with the Rebels? Or had she been hurt in that hard fall? I felt like a fly trapped on the wrong side of a windowpane.

It was a short night, too, because at first dawn the next day the firing commenced again. At first all the officers in Harpers Ferry tried to keep routine. But it was impossible for us to concentrate, and soon enough they gave up. They left us be, with cranky orders to "stay put." We knew they wanted us handy. I expected we'd be called to head out over the pontoon bridge and provide reinforcements any minute.

It was foolish, but some of us climbed out on the roof of our quarters house. From our hillside perch, we could see across to Elk Ridge easily. We could mark the Rebel approach along the ridge by watching the lines of thin blue smoke rise out of the treetops. Only when they got toward Maryland Heights proper, right across the river, and Sergeant Hailey hollered at us, did we retreat back inside.

"I can't sit cooped up in here," Rusty complained, and for once, I agreed with him. Sergeant Hailey had only ordered us off the roof, so we went down to the street. Behind the dubious protection of the armory ruins we found other troopers congregated in huddles like old folks after church, sharing information as it became available.

"A goodly force of Rebels has hit our men! They're trying to drive them back down Maryland Heights," someone said with an air of certainty.

"Randolph, I've seen the breastworks up on that cliff," I muttered. "They looked pretty flimsy." I wondered how the boys crouched behind them felt. And I couldn't help wondering what was going on in the little house at Lock Thirty-Six, almost directly below. How was Mrs. Sutter coping with the thunder? Who was taking care of the children if Mahalia was out?

All morning reports were that the Yankees were holding their own, and we felt somewhat cheered. But by mid-day the first wounded came back into town, and as the afternoon wore on more Federals came streaming across the bridge to Harpers Ferry. Most of them weren't hurt, just scared.

There had been some Ohio and Maryland and Rhode Island boys up there, but the center of the Yankee line had been raw New Yorkers, green recruits who panted out stories of their first battle.

"Colonel Sherrill, he got hit in the face. Mangled his jaw somethin' awful."

"We didn't turn tail! The officers ordered a retreat—"

"Nobody had expected an attack from the north. Cussed fools. The big guns weren't positioned right. The artillery was useless."

They tried to talk big, now that they were away and safe, but in the powder-stained faces I still saw fear. From the snatches of talk came a picture of scared boys skedaddling, scrambling down that rocky cliff as best they could. A few of our boys made half-hearted mutters about the infantry. But just a few.

"The cavalry will be called out for sure, now," Randolph said. I agreed.

But we weren't.

By late afternoon everyone in town knew that a total withdrawal from Maryland Heights had been ordered. The big guns, which had been about useless, were spiked and shoved off the cliffs so the Rebs wouldn't get them. All the Yankees in Maryland came pouring back over the pontoon bridge to Harpers Ferry, leaving Maryland Heights to the enemy.

We were just taking in that knowledge when a new piece of information raced through town. Unresisted, more Confederate troops had occupied Loudon Heights, across the Shenandoah River to the south.

We'd had enough of watching, and congregated with our mess back at the quarters house. "Randolph, don't you think they better be taking us out of here?" I couldn't help asking, low, so no one else could hear.

By that time, even Randolph was looking a mite rattled. "I expect so, Sol. We can still get out by heading west, over Bolivar Heights."

The rest of us thought so too, and we didn't even fix supper, waiting for our orders to ride. But they didn't come. Instead, in early evening, word came that more Confederates had been seen less than a mile west of the main Federal defenses on the low rise of Bolivar Heights.

That news settled in my stomach like a cold ball. Harpers Ferry was surrounded. Worse, the Rebels held all the high ground. We were in the bottom of a bowl.

We didn't talk much after that. We were caught between a buzzard and a hawk. The dullest among us knew Harpers Ferry was as defensible as the bottom of a well.

We were trapped.

CHAPTER TWELVE

I don't think I slept at all that night, and I don't think the rest of the boys did either. We had nothing to do but lie in the dark stillness, knowing the Rebels were out there. And if that wasn't bad enough, I still saw Mahalia's face every time I closed my eyes. How did she feel, knowing we were penned in? Did she have any guilt about me at all?

In the morning I borrowed a pair of field glasses, and for a while watched the little gray figures plainly visible on the crags of Maryland Heights and Loudon Heights. Morning came and went and with the exception of musket fire every now and again, more pesky than actually troublesome, the Confederates were quiet. It was a spooky day, though, because over the mountain passes from the east, somewhere beyond Elk Ridge, drifted the distant thunder of artillery. The entire Confederate army wasn't training their sights on us after all, because another battle was underway. The not knowing was enough to make a man mad.

The Federal artillery on Bolivar Heights tried to dislodge the Rebels on Loudon Heights, but they were out of range. The Confederates had managed to drag some of their own cannon to the crest of Loudon Heights, and midafternoon they began lobbing shots across the Shenandoah at us. They were poorly positioned, and the balls fell short. But I figured the Confederates were smart enough to fix that soon enough. I went back inside.

When I had thought about fighting, I had pictured the actual *doing*, and wondered how I would stand up in a battle. I hadn't known to worry about the hours of thin waiting, knowing a bombardment would come from an enemy too far away to strike back at. Some of the fellows wrote letters home, or tried to read from their testaments. Some of the others started muttering bitter words like siege and surrender and prisoner of war. I didn't see any way out either.

Shelling continued off and on until dusk and then dwindled away again. "They're still getting their guns into position," someone said, and it seemed likely. "I guess the real bombardment won't begin until tomorrow." It didn't bring the relief of a reprieve, only the frustration of facing another sleepless night.

Our room faced Maryland Heights, and we had been forbidden to light candles. Just as fellows were starting to stretch out on their blankets Sergeant Hailey came looking for me. "Hargreave! Colonel Davis is outside. He wants to see you, right now."

I couldn't guess why he'd summon me now. On the sidewalk I found not only Colonel Davis and Major Corliss waiting, but a couple of other cavalry officers I vaguely recognized. They all looked grim, and they didn't make any explanations. Colonel Davis was sucking on a cigar but he hurled it into the street when I clattered out the door. "Come with us," he barked, before I even had a chance to salute. He took off so fast I had to scurry to keep up.

They led me to another private house on High Street. Colonel Davis strode right up the steps and banged on the door himself. After a moment, an aide answered.

"We're here to see Colonel Miles," Colonel Davis announced.

"He's not expecting you—"

"We're here anyway," Davis said. "Tell him his cavalry commanders wish to see him. Immediately."

The aide looked at me funny as we came in. "He's with me," Colonel Davis snapped. The aide kept his mouth shut.

We were shown into the dining room. Heavy black cloth draped the windows, and several lamps had been lit. I recognized Colonel Miles, the garrison commander, sitting with another infantry officer. Colonel Miles was wearing only one hat, I was glad to see.

"Have a seat, gentlemen," he said. Although it wasn't hot in the room, he mopped his face with a kerchief. "Well. What do you wish to see me about?"

"Colonel Miles, we don't like our situation," Colonel Davis said, real plain. "We're in a bad spot here—"

Miles interrupted. "It is true we find ourselves in difficult straits. I want you all to know I sent a message this morning, by three separate couriers, to General McClellan with the main body of the Federal army, last known to be near Frederick. I asked him to send reinforcements—"

In the chair next to me, Colonel Davis made a stifled sound. I dared a glance at him and saw a look on his face I had never seen before. It was kind of like the time at drill he heard Gillis and Rusty complain about his being Southern. Only worse. His body was rigid. I knew he was not just worried. He was very angry.

"My orders," Colonel Miles went on, "are to hold Harpers Ferry and Bolivar Heights as long as possible. I believe we can hold out another twenty-four hours."

"Another twenty-four hours!" Major Corliss exclaimed. "Colonel, if the Rebs open their big guns tomorrow, we won't last another two hours. They had all day to tighten their position."

"Colonel Miles, Colonel Ford, I am going to be blunt," Colonel Davis said. "It was a mistake to withdraw from Maryland Heights—"

Ford, the infantry officer, got real red in the face. "Sir, you presume!" he said angrily. "I was in command of that post. You can't know—"

"I know that too many troops were held in reserve, and never put in the fight," Davis snapped. "I'm not saying it was all your fault, Ford, because I don't believe you got the support and direction you needed. But it shouldn't have happened that way."

"You are insolent!" Ford huffed, but he sank back in his chair. I was already pressed back on mine like a woodtick on a dog. I still had no idea why I had been summoned, and it was mighty uncomfortable to hear officers saying such things to each other.

Then Miles tried to grab back control of the conversation. "Maryland Heights is inconsequential. My orders pertain to Harpers Ferry and Bolivar Heights only. I am to hold—"

Davis didn't even let him finish. "Maryland Heights is not inconsequential! If Maryland Heights had been defended, we wouldn't be in this trap. Surely your orders were not meant to be interpreted so literally! You can't defend this garrison without Maryland Heights, and you practically handed it over to the enemy."

"Colonel Davis, you are in danger of insubordination," Miles warned. I thought that was generous of him, actually.

"Yes sir, I am. But I wanted to make things very clear. As we see it," he gestured to the other cavalry officers, "you, as garrison commander, have jeopardized your men by evacuating Maryland Heights, and at the same time failing to evacuate your command here before the western escape route was sealed. We made a formal request for cavalry action yesterday afternoon, which was summarily denied. Since that time, you have sat on your hands while the Confederates tightened the noose around our necks. You have left this garrison with no hope but to surrender."

The room was silent. Miles mopped his face again but didn't find anything to say.

Colonel Davis's voice was a little quieter when he went on. "Colonel Miles, we cavalrymen have discussed the situation at length. And we are proposing to break out of Harpers Ferry. Tonight."

My mouth dropped open.

"There is no hope for the infantry," Davis went on. "None. But with horses... we can move quickly. We just might be able to get out."

"You can't be serious!"

"I assure you I am."

"I can't consider such a preposterous proposal. We are facing a siege. I need the cavalry—"

Colonel Davis shook his head. "Cavalry can't defend this garrison against an artillery siege! The cavalry can be of no help to Harpers Ferry at this juncture. The only good we can do now is try to keep those horses and their riders and their equipment out of Rebel hands. The Confederacy is desperate for horses, and we've got fourteen hundred trapped here—"

Miles suddenly slammed his fist on the table. "I won't permit it! Your plan is wild and impractical. Wild and impractical!" He pushed to his feet, panting with fury, and it occurred to me that the wildest thing in the room was him. "Your plan is extremely hazardous. It could only result in high losses—"

"High losses! Colonel Miles, *everything* is going to be lost if we stay here! Any escape attempt, even if it means a bloody running fight all the way to the Pennsylvania border, is preferable to sitting penned up here! Are we to calmly hand over all of our mounts and equipment, not to mention our boys, to the Rebel cavalry?" Davis was on his feet too, pacing back and forth like a caged cat.

Miles glared at him. "What you propose is impossible—"

"It is a chance!" Colonel Davis yelled. "Even a slim chance is more than we have if we stay here!"

"I will not allow it," Miles said, in a voice like ice. He sat back down and began sorting through papers, as if he had already moved on to other business. "Permission denied."

I held my breath, and I think everyone else in the room did too. Slowly, Colonel Davis crossed his arms. "I am not asking for your permission," he said, real cold. "With your permission or not, I am taking my men out of here. Tonight."

I looked around the room. Each cavalryman was wearing a tight expression. I could tell they were all behind Davis. Colonel Ford, the infantry commander, was gaping. Colonel Miles was staring at Davis with a look that made me pity him, poor old man.

Finally he sagged in his chair. He hid his face in his hands, and for a horrified moment I thought he was going to cry. But when he raised it again his expression was set. "Binney!" he called to his aide. "Bring me the maps from the other room." When Binney appeared with the maps, Miles spread one open and pinned the corners down with books. "Now. Let's consider the route."

Things weren't settled that quickly, though, because a whole lot of haggling about the route commenced. "Hargreave, come here," Colonel Davis said, and I finally realized why I'd been brought. Of them all, I was the one who had explored the terrain across the river. Colonel Davis had even brought a couple of my own sketched maps. He and Colonel Miles argued about this or that, and then Colonel Davis would say, "Well Hargreave? Is that ford passable in the dark?" Or, "Is this road as circuitous as it looks?" Finally the officers decided that we would cross the pontoon bridge over the Potomac toward Maryland Heights, then head north toward Sharpsburg on the Maryland side.

Colonel Ford watched those negotiations in silence. When things were settled, he said, timid-like, "Colonel Miles? Perhaps the infantry—"

"No!" Colonel Miles bellowed. "The infantry and artillery, every last man, will be at Bolivar Heights tomorrow. This garrison will not be surrendered without a fight. And none but the cavalry are to know of this planned escape attempt. It would cause a stampede."

I don't know if Ford agreed with him, or if he just didn't have as much spine as Colonel Davis. But he slumped back in his chair, silent.

"You couldn't make it anyway," Davis said to him quietly. "We need speed, man." Ford nodded.

Before we left, Colonel Miles made a point of issuing a written order for the cavalry to leave Harpers Ferry at nine o'clock that evening. "I can give you no other instruction than to force your way through the enemy lines and join our own army," he said, kind of cool, I thought. Like the whole plan was his idea.

Colonel Davis and the other cavalrymen barely acknowledged him as they got up to leave. I trailed after them. We were out the door before I heard someone call, "Wait!"

We turned around, and saw Colonel Ford and the aide, Binney. "Good luck, sirs," Binney said smartly, and hit as snappy a salute as I'd ever seen. Colonel Ford followed suit, looking a funny cross between respectful and jealous. Poor foot-slogger, I thought. If Ford had handled the mess up on Maryland Heights badly, as Colonel Davis had suggested, he was going to pay dearly for it.

The officers scattered then, each to rouse their own men. Colonel Davis came down to our barracks house with me. "I want to see all my officers," he told the sentry posted at the door. And to me, "You can join your company for now, Hargreave, but I'll want you later."

Upstairs, my messmates mobbed me, wanting to know what was up. I shut the door, and everybody sat on the blankets while I told the story.

"Whooee!" someone whistled, when I got to the part about the escape. "A breakout!"

"We'll never make it," someone else fretted.

"Better than getting captured. I wasn't fancy on spending the rest of the war in some Reb prison."

"Do you think we can do it?" Randolph asked me.

"Colonel Davis does," I said honestly, although I didn't know that I should mention how he had said so: *Any escape attempt, even if it means a bloody running fight all the way to the Pennsylvania border, is preferable to sitting penned up here!* As for me, well, I had no idea. But I liked his idea better than sitting and waiting for us to get shelled to pieces, or surrendered.

Then Gillis, mean, stupid Gillis, had to speak his piece. "You boys are forgettin' something," he cut in. His voice was low. "What makes you so sure Colonel Davis ain't leading us into a trap?"

The only sound in the room was a mouse scrabbling in the straw for stray crumbs. Then Randolph said, "Why would he do that?"

"Because he's Southern, you dolt," Rusty said. "Don't he have two brothers in the Rebel army? Didn't Sol say he near on to mutinied Colonel Miles? Colonel Miles is his superior officer. It ain't right, what he done."

"He did it because Colonel Miles is acting like a fool," I protested.

"Like a fool?" Gillis asked. "Or like a good Federal officer? I tell you, boys, I ain't following no Southerner right into Reb lines in the dark. It's crazy. I say Davis has been biding his time, just waiting for this kind of opportunity. Now he's got his chance. He wants to deliver all of us straight to the Confederates." For a moment no one answered. I could see that a couple of the fellows were thinking that over.

Suddenly, I felt hot anger boil up inside. I'd had all I could take of turning away from people who pushed me: Betsy Lee, Elisha, Mahalia. And now Gillis.

I did something I'd read about in books but never seen anyone actually do before. I grabbed the front of Gillis's shirt and pulled him right in front of my face. "That's a lie!" I yelled. "You're the dolt! We're already in the trap! If we stay we won't have any chance at all! Colonel Davis is man enough to give us a chance, and I for one am going to follow him. If you want to stay here and sulk, fine! Go ahead! But if you say one more word against Colonel Davis I'll—"

"You'll what?" Gillis finally got over his surprise and pulled free. "You want to take me on, Hargreave? Is that what you want?"

I dove at him and we crashed over in a rough embrace. Before the brawl could really begin, though, a cold stream of water caught us both in the face. "Stop it!" Randolph cried, in a voice I'd never heard. He was clutching his canteen. "We're not here to fight each other. Now leave be. Leave be!"

We separated slowly, still tense and glaring, each ready to throw a fist if the other made a move. But before that could happen, the door banged open and Sergeant Hailey stuck his head inside.

"Grab your things and head for the stable, boys," he said. "We're going for a ride."

My few possessions were packed in a blanket roll and saddlebag in about two seconds. I **was** disappointed to see that Gillis and Rusty, after a long look to each other, packed up too. I wouldn't have minded leaving them behind at all.

CHAPTER THIRTEEN

We formed up in a column of twos on Shenandoah Street. At the head of the line was our flag bearer, carrying our standard. It was blue silk with gold fringe, and had an eagle and "8th N.Y. Cavalry" painted on it. It was hard to see, in the dark. But it was a glory to know it was there.

In addition to Colonel Davis's Eighth New York Cavalry, and Major Corliss's "College Cavaliers," there were the Twelfth Illinois Cavalry and smaller units of Maryland troopers. Like the Colonel had said, there were about fourteen hundred horsemen in Harpers Ferry that night. Every cavalry commander had elected to follow him.

It took a while to get everyone jostled into place. Colonel Davis went up and down the file, repeating basic instructions in a calm tone: "There will be no talking. Maintain your intervals." I also heard Major Corliss talking to his boys. "Keep your heads," he told them. "Whether we succeed or not, it is a great thing we are attempting." Then he added that by dawn they would be free men, prisoners, or dead—"in Pennsylvania, on the way to Richmond, or in Hell." We all knew which one we were aiming for.

While we were waiting, a man on foot came out of the shadows. "Here, boy," he muttered, pressing something into my hand—a pouch of tobacco. It was the regimental sutler, and to my wonder he went down the line, giving away every last bit he had.

Finally, when my stomach was about tied in knots from waiting, we were ready to start. Colonel Davis rode at the head of the column. With him was a local who knew the area named Tom Noakes and a scout who had recently sniffed out the lay of the Confederate army—and me, since I had mapped part of the road just days before. "Stay close," the Colonel told me, and I figured there was no order I was more likely to follow. We were all expecting a bloody time of it. Truth to tell, I was scared. But I was more scared of letting the Colonel down than getting shot by the Rebels.

We crossed the pontoon bridge at a walk. I figured the wild water rushing against the rocks below covered our noise. The rapids gave me thought of Randolph, who didn't take much to water crossings, but I reckoned we both had bigger things to think about. I could see the Rebel campfires twinkling on Maryland Heights, just ahead.

My heart was pounding when we eased from the bridge, because Colonel Davis had expected to meet Confederate pickets blocking the road at the base of the mountain. To our surprise, there were none. I pointed the way left onto the narrow road that wound to the west around Maryland Heights and then north toward Sharpsburg.

"Now we need to fly," the Colonel whispered. It would take about two hours to get the whole column across the bridge, and we had to make time afterwards. We kicked our horses into a full-out hard gallop and headed north.

Just when I most needed my wits, I thought again about Mahalia. After all, I was practically within a shout of Lock Thirty-Six. For all I knew, she was out prowling the night herself, with her Loudon County Scouts.

It was about then I realized that this breakout was more than a chance to escape bombardment or Rebel prison, for

1862 Brady photograph of Harpers Ferry, orginally published in *Harpers Weekly* in October 1862. This view shows the U.S. Armory grounds along the Potomac shore in Harpers Ferry. Note the beginnings of the pontoon bridge across the Potomac, which the cavalry crossed on the night of their breakout, near the damaged railroad bridge. Loudon Heights, across the Shenandoah River, is visible to the right.

Harpers Ferry National Historical Park,
National Park Service

me. For me it was a chance to redeem myself, my army—to keep those confounded bushwhackers from getting the last laugh. Lordy be, if we could only make it! I took pleasure in the picture I formed of the Confederate officers, when Harpers Ferry fell, finding out that somehow all the horses they had been hankering after were gone!

But it was too early to enjoy such thoughts, and I quick yanked my brain back to the job at hand. The Colonel set a killing pace. Suddenly every minute of the hard drills we had endured, and grumbled at, were justified. I even had to be grateful for Mahalia's pointers.

There was no moon. In the woods the night was so thick black that I could keep my proper interval only by listening for the tiny rattle of the Colonel's saber, and watching for sparks that came from his horse's shoes striking the rocky road. Sometimes I got the feeling we were miles ahead of the other men. Other times, they came up on us too fast in the darkness, and nearly ran us over. Then I heard the stifled mutters of some tall swearing.

About twelve miles from Harpers Ferry we came up the Hagerstown Road to the little village of Sharpsburg. We came round a bend and suddenly the darkness was spotted with a hundred flickering lights. Before I realized they were Confederate campfires, a sheet of flame exploded in the night. Hail rattled in the air around my head: bullets.

There wasn't even time to panic. Colonel Davis wheeled his mount around, and the rest of us did too. There was confusion as we backtracked half a mile or so, trying to avoid those coming behind and passing muttered directions back down the file. The Reb outpost we'd startled tossed a couple of shells our way, but they were way off course, and didn't do any harm.

Colonel Davis pulled his guides over for a lightening-quick consultation. "That's too strong an outpost to penetrate," he breathed. "Options?"

"Go back to the fork and take the west road," I offered.

The scout shook his head. "The Reb line stretches that way. We'd be likely to hit just as strong a force."

"I say skirt around toward Falling Waters, then try to find a weaker point to pierce their lines," Tom Noakes said. "But we're not going to find it on any road. Colonel, I've hunted every inch of this county. I think our best chance is overland until we get at least as far as Hagerstown."

"Do it," Colonel Davis ordered. In less time than it takes to tell, the entire column was creeping into the woods.

It seemed like I held my breath for the next few hours of riding, and that every other man did too. But the time for being scared was past. *Trust,* Colonel Davis had preached once, and that was all we had left. We'd already trusted him with our very lives. Now we had to trust Noakes, who led us through woods and fields, sometimes threading our way in between the very camps where our enemies lay sleeping, so close we could smell the coffee and sowbelly left from their suppers and see the flicker of dying campfires. We had to trust our comrades to be as silent and cautious as ourselves. And we had to trust our horses. As the night wore on, and a powerful weariness began pulling at me, I finally learned to give that trust over to Cinder. Even when I nodded off in the saddle, she kept going as if she knew what I needed her to do.

We emerged from a deep woods onto a road again just before dawn. "Gentlemen, I give you the Hagerstown Turnpike," Noakes said in a low tone, with a gallant flourish.

There was satisfaction in Colonel Davis's voice. "Well done, man," he said. But while I was ready to whoop with relief, realizing we had crossed through the Rebel lines, his brain was still working. "We're probably spread out for ten miles," he mused, twisting in the saddle. "And there's still a good chance for trouble—"

Before he could even finish his sentence he got proved right. The army scout, well used to danger, jerked his head. "Colonel, I hear somethin'—" He gestured up the road toward Hagerstown.

Without a word the Colonel rounded us back into the trees. We plunged into the dark shadows. Word was whispered back the line to stay put. I slid off Cinder and listened.

At first, all I could hear were a few vireos and chickadees, just starting to warm up their before-dawn chorus. Then we all heard something else—a rumbling sound. Any soldier who'd ever heard that particular rumble remembered it, because it was the welcome sound of a heavy wagon train, burdened with supplies.

"That's bound to be Confederate," Colonel Davis whispered. "On its way to supply the army we just rode through. Is there a junction between this spot and the Confederate line? Hargreave?"

"I didn't get up this far, sir," I answered, with deep regret.

"Noakes?"

"Well, about a quarter mile back. The left fork runs back into the Rebel army. The right would take you to Greencastle." Greencastle, I recalled, was in Pennsylvania.

I was close enough to the Colonel to sense him chew that information over. Then, "I want the Eighth New York to follow me, quick," he ordered, and we passed the word.

When the wagon train reached the fork in the road Colonel Davis was waiting for it, with his regiment behind. There was barely enough gray light to make out the first wagon as it creaked into sight, but we could see the lantern hung near the seat.

"Halt!" Colonel Davis cried. "Are you boys looking for the Confederate line?" His Mississippi drawl seemed even richer than usual. And the musty light blurred the color of his uniform.

"Yes suh," came the answer from the head mule driver. He sounded sleepy.

"Good," Colonel Davis said. "I'm Colonel Davis, sent out to warn you of Federal cavalry ahead. A force broke out of Harpers Ferry last night. Your orders are now to proceed north. Turn off here. I'll have a few of my men lead the way."

And so, with Yankee cavalrymen showing the way, the tired drivers obediently turned and rumbled north, away from their own army.

Colonel Davis sent us along to "lead" the wagons. About ten minutes later we heard some shooting behind us, but it didn't last long. "Wonder what that's all about," one of the drivers said to me, still sounding more groggy than interested.

"Couldn't say," I mumbled. Unlike the colonel's, my accent was a dead giveaway. I learned later that there was an escort of Confederate cavalry with the wagon train. When they realized the head of the train was turning right at the fork, they came pounding up wanting to know why. Colonel Davis had the Twelfth Illinois charge them out of the woods, and the Reb riders got driven off quick.

We made a couple of miles before daylight showed the drivers the true color of our uniforms. The fellow I was riding beside had been half asleep. When his wagon hit a rut and he was jostled awake, he caught sight of me. The look on his face was something I want to remember all my days.

"Say, what's the name of your outfit?" he stammered.

I grinned, sociable-like. "Eighth New York."

"What's that?" he exclaimed. Twisting around on his seat, he saw a long line of Yankee riders, flanking each side of the supply train. I heard cursing of the kind I won't repeat.

Those drivers, realizing they were prisoners, tried every way they knew how to stop the train. They were loyal Confederates, and figured if they could delay the train, or make a commotion, the Rebels might overtake us. One fellow got down and started unhitching his mules. The driver I was guarding, who was carrying shells, set fire to the straw they were packed in.

"Tarnation!" I cried. I flung myself from Cinder and beat out the flames. I was glad to see Sergeant Hailey as I emptied my canteen on them for good measure. "Don't try that again," he warned the Reb. And to me, "Ride with pistol cocked, Private. Shoot if necessary." The driver turned sullen but settled down.

Truth to tell, we couldn't yet enjoy our success. Colonel Davis had taken a mighty chance, and we were pretty tense that the Rebels would come back for us yet. We rode along with ears straining to hear a charge coming up behind us.

It never came.

What we heard instead was a distant booming to the south, rolling over the miles, continuous. The Confederates were shelling Harpers Ferry. I wondered how quickly the surrender would come, and when the Confederates would realize the cavalry had escaped. I wondered when Mahalia would hear that news.

We reached the safe, loyal town of Greencastle about nine o'clock that morning. We'd captured forty wagons packed with Confederate flour and ammunition, along with several hundred stout mules and about a hundred Rebel prisoners—the drivers plus some infantry stragglers who'd thought to hitch a ride and were asleep in the wagons.

The townsfolk tumbled out to the street chirping like magpies. We told the story. At first they couldn't believe what we'd done: broke out of Harpers Ferry, slipped through the Confederate lines, and captured the wagon train, all in twelve hours and without a single man lost.

Randolph found me in the crowd. He was hungry and tired and saddle-sore but happy. "We did it, Sol, we did it!" His face was shining.

I saw Gillis nearby, and edged the mare over. "Hey Gillis! You got anything to say now?" He didn't.

Then Colonel Davis, who had ridden back to check on the rear of the line, cantered up. The civilians started clapping. We New York boys, who could claim him as our own Colonel, mobbed the man, whooping and hollering like kids just let out of school. The Colonel laughed, grabbed the standard from the flag bearer and thrust it up toward the sky. And my heart, which had seen nothing but hurt for so long, started coming back to life.

CHAPTER FOURTEEN

Everyone had their story to tell after that night. One company of the Twelfth Illinois had turned right instead of left when they got across the pontoon bridge, and ended up running into a Confederate patrol in Sandy Hook. They got shot at and galloped back the right direction. One fellow, who left the line to relieve himself, got so close to a Confederate camp he heard a picket humming under his breath. He said he was about to harmonize when he recognized "Dixie."

Colonel Davis had given us something to glory in, and we did. It was a good thing to have, too, because what came soon after didn't give much cause for cheering.

General Lee had sent three divisions—fourteen thousand men, led by no other than the mighty Stonewall Jackson—to capture Harpers Ferry. We found that out later. Jackson had a reputation for fierce fighting, and we barely got out in time. We broke out on Sunday night. On Monday morning, at first light, fifty cannon let loose at Harpers Ferry.

It was more than the garrison could stand. Harpers Ferry was surrendered before we even got to Greencastle. Colonel Miles was wounded by a gun fired after the white flags were raised. He died the next day.

When the Confederates captured Harpers Ferry, they captured seventy-three artillery pieces, thirteen thousand rifles and muskets, and twelve thousand and five hundred prisoners, all infantry and artillery. It was their biggest booty of the war. Rightly or wrongly, most of the men taken prisoner were bitter and blamed Colonel Miles. Some say he sold his army to the enemy. Some say that mortal shell was fired at Miles deliberately by a Yankee gunner.

But that was just the beginning. After Jackson captured Harpers Ferry, he hiked his men back to the main army and two days later, at Sharpsburg, came the Battle of Antietam Creek.

The Eighth New York Cavalry was there. But truth to tell, I'm not yet able to write much about it. I can tell the numbers: folks say there were more than *twenty-two thousand* men killed or wounded. It was a day Hell surely came to earth, and I pray the like of that never comes again. I was there. But the things I saw that day are just too fierce to write about, at least for a while.

Besides, that was the day I lost Randolph. We were rounding up stragglers, after the battle. One pulled a pistol and shot Randolph straight through the heart. When I got to him, and knew he was gone, I put my face down and bawled. He'll never eat his mama's ham and dumplings again, or find a sweetheart. The only comfort I can take is that it came quick. That—and that he'd had his night of glory, like the rest of us. He died a true soldier.

After the battle, my regiment made camp near Hagerstown. A lot of the boys fell into a funk. The Confederates had been driven back across the river to Virginia, but lots of people said we should have been able to whip them once and for all, and end the war. As September turned into October, we began to realize that the war was far from being over, and it made for some heavy hearts.

Randolph's death ripped a hole in me. But at least I could grieve Randolph clean. I knew he was dead, and gone for good, and I knew that we hadn't had any unfinished business before he died. It wasn't like that with Mahalia. I kept thinking about her, and how our business had not been finished off clean like it should have been.

Things were quiet for a couple of weeks. It got so I couldn't get Mahalia out of my mind. The picture of her riding off with Elisha, and all the words I wanted to say to her, kept bubbling up stronger and stronger. Finally I went to see Captain de Vries.

Captain de Vries, the boys said, had been scared enough to wet himself the night we broke out of Harpers Ferry. He'd come through it, though, and Antietam too. I didn't want to hate him. That day, I tried to be my most respectful.

It got me nothing. "Permission denied, Hargreave," he said real cool, when I asked for a pass. "The entire company is confined to camp."

Then I did something I'd never done before. I broke regulations and went on to find Colonel Davis on my own.

He was in his tent. It was not quite as fine a setting as he'd had in Harpers Ferry! But it was the first time I'd talked to him face-to-face since the breakout. I was glad to see him.

He was polishing a bridle, and motioned me to sit on a camp stool he'd scrounged up. "Hargreave. What can I do for you?"

"I don't have permission to be here, sir." I figured I best get that out in the open. "But things are pretty quiet here, at least right now, and... well, I wondered if you needed any more scouting done. Sketching."

He regarded me intently. "I appreciate your offer, Hargreave. What exactly are you asking me for?"

I looked him in the eye. "Well, I'd like permission to leave camp for a day. I have some unfinished business in Sandy Hook."

"What did Captain de Vries say?"

"Captain de Vries said no."

The Colonel didn't speak for a moment, just sat there rubbing the smooth leather in his fingers. I wondered if he recalled having this conversation with me once before. Then he said, "You may go tomorrow."

I was relieved. We could get called away from western Maryland at any time, and the thought of moving on without saying my mind to Mahalia Sutter was more than I could live with.

"I'll tell Captain de Vries you are on my errand. But I can not do this again. Captain de Vries needs your respect. Is that understood?"

"Yes sir."

I saluted and started to turn away, but he called me back. "Private Hargreave."

"Sir?"

"I saw Private McCallister's name on the lists. I'm sorry. I know he was your friend."

I took a deep breath. "Thank you, sir. He was a good man." Calling Randolph that was the highest tribute I could pay my friend.

"I know, son," the Colonel said. I went away figuring that Davis calling me "son" paid me the equal.

The little city of Hagerstown is only about twenty miles from Harpers Ferry. The roads were crowded in spots, with supply trains and ambulance wagons still evacuating the sick and wounded. But at least all the traffic belonged to the Union army. I made good time. Such good time, in fact, that I got to Lock Thirty-Six before I'd figured out exactly what I was going to say.

The kids were in the yard, and galloped over when they saw me. "Hey, Solomon!" Even little Lizzie hugged my legs.

"I need to see your sister," I told them, feeling hurt twist in my chest. I didn't have younger brothers and sisters of my own, and I'd enjoyed being around these kids. "You run on."

When I knocked on the door, Phoebe answered. "If it isn't Private Hargreave! Why, we heard all you Yankee cavalry had ridden out of these parts. Right through the lines, they say! We surely didn't expect to be seeing you again—"

"Yes, I'm sure," I said, real rude. Her manner, which had always seemed so lady-like, didn't ring true anymore. I'd never noticed that before, and I suddenly wondered if pretty Miss Phoebe had known about Mahalia all along, and had been laughing at me behind all her sweet talk. Without doubt, I decided. "Where's Mahalia?"

"Why, sir, your tone!" she pouted, but let me inside, which was a good thing, because I wasn't above pushing her aside to get past. "She's out back—"

Mrs. Sutter came down the stairs, leaning on the railing like she couldn't quite stand up by herself. "Phoebe, who's there? Is that your pa?"

"No, Mama. You go back upstairs."

"It's Private Hargreave, ma'am," I said, since she was peering at me, and didn't move.

"Have you seen my husband?"

"No ma'am. I'm sorry," I said, and I meant it. She slowly disappeared back upstairs.

I turned my back on Phoebe and went outside. I found Mahalia in the stable, squatting over a dead chicken she was plucking. There was a pan of steaming water beside her, and another for the innards, and a bag for the pinfeathers. Her fingers were flying but they stopped when she realized someone had come in. "Solomon!"

"Surprised to see me?" I asked, in a real hard voice.

"I'm glad to see you. What with the big battle and all, I didn't know if you were safe—"

All the hurt and anger I'd been carrying these past weeks came flying out like steam from a teakettle. "You can stop pretending, Mahalia! I just came to let you know that I know all about it. About you and the Loudon County Scouts."

"What do you mean?"

"I know about you riding with them! You are a mean and selfish person. I don't give a jigger who you ride with, but there was no call to suck me into it. What did you think, you could trick me into giving you some information? Was that the plan?"

Mahalia put the chicken down. Her face had closed off, so I couldn't read her expression. She wiped her hands on her trousers and pushed up to her feet. "I don't know what you mean," she said finally.

For some reason, her calm tone just made me angrier. "Mahalia, stop lying! I *saw* you! I saw you." The sudden tiny frown on her face made me give a bitter laugh. "Ha, you didn't know that, did you? So there's no sense denying it. I saw you."

"Where?"

"At Zeke Cherry's place."

"I've never been to Zeke Cherry's—"

"By God, Mahalia, I was there! I was up on the hill, watching. Oh, you hid it pretty good, I'll agree to that. I didn't even realize it was you, that night at Torrisons'! But your hat fell off in the skirmish at the inn, didn't it? Mahalia, I saw you! With Elisha. I saw your hair."

She looked like she'd just been punched in the gut. She leaned back against the stable wall and bowed her head.

I wanted to keep angry. But seeing her like that, not cocky or anything, made the hurt come out instead. "How could you do that to me?" I asked, and all of a sudden my voice was scrawny. "I trusted you, Mahalia! I thought we were friends!" I felt a funny lump rise in my throat. "I told you things I'd never told anyone before. How could you lie to me?"

"She didn't lie to you."

That voice came from behind me. I whirled around and saw Phoebe. She smiled at the shocked look on my face. "Do forgive me for intruding, but I couldn't stand out there and listen to any more of this. My sister is many things, Mr. Hargreave, but she is not a liar."

I think my mouth was hanging open. Mahalia didn't move. But real quiet she said, "Phoebe, why didn't you tell me?"

"Why didn't I tell you? Because I shouldn't have had to tell you. You should have been a part of it yourself."

"Wait a minute," I stammered, looking from one to the other. "Do you mean to say...." I couldn't even form the words.

Phoebe sniffed. "You Yankees are a particularly dull-witted lot, Mr. Hargreave. And you have a thing or two to learn about Southern women."

"It was *you?*"

"You should have told me," Mahalia interrupted. "Corbin was my brother too."

"You certainly never acted like it!" Phoebe snapped. "Did you ever support him in his cause?"

"I didn't *not* support him! But Crimus, Phoebe, this is not a Confederate house—"

"It should have been! Just because Mama married a fool the second time around doesn't mean we're not still Fosdicks. And Fosdicks are not Yankees."

I was still trying to figure it all out. "How did you manage to keep it a secret?"

She looked at me like I was stupid. "It wasn't particularly hard. I haven't been riding with the Scouts all the time, just every now and then. It's for the people's sake, really. They get a glimpse of this Sutter face and they think Corbin's still alive. They think he's invincible. They think the Confederacy is invincible. All I have to do is change my clothes at my grandmother's cabin—"

Granny Fosdick. Of course. I remembered all too well her cutting tongue, and her fretful 'I want Phoebe!' the afternoon I'd been there with Mahalia. I also remembered the scolding Mahalia had taken from her, and it made me angry.

But Mahalia was thinking of someone else. "You shouldn't be taking these chances," she said. "What if something happens to you too? What will that do to Mama?"

"Mahalia, I'm doing this for the cause! I'm fighting a war—"

"Maybe your own family could use your help!"

"Maybe you should remember who your father was!"

I was wondering if I was going to have to break up a brawl then and there when we got interrupted by the blare of a boathorn. Mahalia stamped her foot with vexation, glaring at her sister, before pushing past to go tend the lock.

Then Phoebe and I were alone. I shook my head. "I can't believe it was you."

Phoebe gave me a look of scorn. "You men are all alike. You see a pretty face and a pretty dress and you assume we're simple-minded, with no thoughts of our own."

I felt like slapping her.

"People like you make it easy for a woman. I developed a delicate constitution. I got fevers, and needed rest." She laughed. "I wasn't ill! I'd just been out all night, and needed to sleep. You never gave it a thought, did you?"

I couldn't defend myself against that, for fact is, it was true.

"I ought to take you prisoner," I muttered instead.

"Would that make you feel good? Taking a woman prisoner? Go ahead. I dare you." She had gotten me again, for she was right—I didn't have it in me. She smiled. "I'd deny it all anyway, and I doubt too many people would believe you." Then she fluttered her eyelashes at me, with a pretty smile, just like the first time I'd met her. "A sweet thing like me?"

"I hope what people would believe is that you're a silly girl who thinks it's a lark to keep company with a bunch of bushwhackers. To you it's all a game—"

"Game!" she cried, all sweetness gone. "I assure you that there are many loyal Confederates in Maryland, and to us, it is no game. I have a cause, the same cause my brother died for. The same cause all my cousins and friends are fighting for, the same one my father would be fighting for if he was alive today. Mahalia doesn't understand that."

"I don't think you're being fair to your sister," I said angrily. "Maybe she values keeping this family fed more than anything else." And then I turned around and walked out. I didn't want to exchange one more word with Phoebe Sutter.

The canalboat was disappearing when I found Mahalia. She had shut the sluice gate but was leaning on the gatepost, just staring down at the water. That look reminded me of the first time I'd ever seen her, and I hurried over. "Are you all right?"

She kicked a stone into the lock. "I'm just thinking."

"About Phoebe."

"No, about Corbin. He's dead for sure, then."

"Well... I guess so. I am sorry, Mahalia." I felt guilty for getting her hopes up before, when I thought I'd seen him. "And I'm sorry that I caused trouble in your family. I sure never meant to do that."

"You didn't do anything. This family had trouble long before you came along."

"I still can't believe it was Phoebe, and not you." It would take me a long time to get used to that idea. "I thought she was such a lady. I mean—" I realized how that sounded in reference to Mahalia, and wished I'd held my tongue.

"Oh, don't fret about it. I never claimed to be a lady."

"I think you are," I said slowly. I was amazed, but it was true. I'd known lots of girls I'd thought were ladies, like Betsy Lee, and Phoebe. I had thought they were everything a lady should be. But I was starting to realize just how wrong I was. Maybe I'd been looking for the wrong things. "I think you are a lady."

Then something else popped into my head. "Almighty!" I gasped, and clapped a hand over my mouth. "My mama would tan my hide if she knew. I believe I cursed at you before, Mahalia. I *am* sorry."

Mahalia almost smiled at that. "Solomon, you are a funny person. I believe I've cussed at you a time or two. I guess we're even."

"Friends?"

"Friends."

Just then the door banged behind us and here came Phoebe, dressed to go walking, looking pretty as ever. "Don't take this unkind, but I don't enjoy your company," she said to me. And to her sister, "I'm going for a walk. Mama's lying down, and I set Clem to watching the little ones. I don't know when I'll be home. If you need to reach me—"

"Phoebe, just *go!*" Mahalia's voice let me know how angry she was at her sister. With a toss of her head, Phoebe crossed the bridge and disappeared down the towpath.

I watched her go, shaking my head like an old man who has just seen some new wonder. "You know, when Mr. Timmerman told me about that horse race you and Phoebe and Corbin had at Maryland Heights, I couldn't picture Phoebe riding rough. I should have tried harder."

"Those were good times." Mahalia sighed, kind of wistful. "We all had a wild streak, I guess. People said we were just like our father. Our real father. Corbin never grew out of it. I guess Phoebe never did either, really. She just hid it under those pretty ways."

"Well, I'm glad you don't hide things," I said. "And I'm glad Phoebe told the truth. It was terrible for me, thinking it was you. It was eating me up inside. I... I've been hating you, these past couple weeks."

"Because you thought I was a secret Confederate?"

"No. I mean, I don't agree with it, but I can respect a person's stand. The thing is, I thought you had lied to me."

"I would never lie to you, Solomon," she said quietly.

"I know," I answered, and knew I'd never doubt it again.

I had the rest of the day free, and I wanted to spend it with Mahalia. A proper gentleman would have asked to take her walking, I guess, but instead I helped her butcher another chicken. Then we fixed supper, and got the kids washed up. To make up for being short with Lizzie when I'd come, I gave her a ride on my shoulders to the pump and back. When Thomas started to fret just as the chicken was frying, Mahalia plunked him in my arms and I held him until she got things dished up. After we ate, I hauled water and we did the dishes.

It was funny, but sharing those chores just seemed right, somehow. A quiet, calm feeling came inside of me, something I'd never felt in all the Sunday afternoons in the

Thorntons' parlor, or taking Betsy Lee to singing school or taffy pulls or anything else. I knew I'd found the place I wanted to be. I think Mahalia knew it too.

We talked about the war, and I told her about Randolph. She told me about hiding in the cellar during the battle for Maryland Heights, trying to keep the kids calm. She told me about her mama, who had gotten worse during the terrible shelling, and who came downstairs twice looking for her dead husband before dinner was even on the table. And we talked about how close I'd come to never knowing the truth about her and Phoebe. It made my skin tingle, just thinking about it.

When the dishes were put away we went back outdoors and sat by the lock. There was a nip in the air, and a few of the maples by the yard were starting to turn. Summer was over.

"You know, I wonder if Elisha went to Lucy because she was with him in her heart," Mahalia said. "I mean, with the Confederacy. I never was, in particular. I never pretended to be. Do you think that's wrong? That a person doesn't choose sides, I mean?"

"No. I think you chose to take care of your family. As for Elisha—" I didn't finished my sentence. There wasn't any point.

"It's going to take me some time to get over it. What happened with Elisha."

"I know."

"The hardest part is knowing he never did really love me. He couldn't have spent time with Lucy if he did."

I thought that over, and decided it made sense. "I don't guess Betsy Lee loved me either, really. She said she did. But it's the same thing. She couldn't have got engaged to someone else so quick."

"You know what I think? I think we should feel sorry for them. They don't know how to treat people."

I smiled at her. I even took her hand. "I think you're right."

It was hard to think about riding off, but I only had a one-day pass. Mahalia understood. She didn't cling or say pitiful things like most women do when a man says good-bye. "I don't suppose we'll be bivouacked so close for much longer," I said, as I swung back to the saddle. "I don't know that I'll be able to visit again before we get new orders."

"After the war, will you come back?"

"Yes," I promised. And then, thinking about all the burdens on her shoulders, and that first day in the Potomac, "Will you be here? Waiting?"

"Yes," she promised, and that was that.

I leaned down from the saddle and touched her lips with mine. Mahalia smiled. It was the first time I'd seen her do that, and do you know, she was downright pretty.

I didn't like leaving her alone to face all her troubles, and I know she didn't like sending me back to the war. But we each had our job to do, and we each knew it. Mahalia didn't cry when I rode away. And I didn't look back.

PILOGUE

My regiment got called away soon after that. We forded the Potomac into Virginia on the first of November. It was a cold, gray day and some of the fellows declared we had finally crossed back into Rebeldom. I knew it took more than a river to mark that line.

I had to leave without settling my score with Elisha Forbes. I'd still like to run into that fellow again. After getting things sorted out with Mahalia, though, I found that didn't matter as much. A war tends to make clear what's most important.

So now we're down here in Virginia, skirmishing with the Rebs and moving farther and farther from home. I can't say I don't feel uneasy about the next big battle shaping up, after what I saw at Antietam Creek. And I can't say I don't get cruel lonesome, with Randolph gone.

But I'm luckier than most. I have a crazy, Mississippi-drawling Colonel I'd follow to Hell and back, if he led the way. He wasn't what I'd expected. But I know I can trust him with my life.

And I have a tough, trouser-wearing girl with sun-yellow hair, waiting for me back at Lock Thirty-Six. She wasn't what I expected, either. But I'm trusting her with my heart.

Author's Note

Solomon Hargreave and his comrades in the Eighth New York Cavalry, and Mahalia Sutter and her family, are fictitious. Their world as portrayed in this story, however, is as close to authentic as possible. Some of the men who belonged to the real Eighth New York Cavalry and other cavalry regiments involved in the breakout from Harpers Ferry left behind diaries or other records, which helped piece together their story. In a few cases, their words were used as dialogue. The Loudon County Scouts are also fictitious, but based on real bands of partisan riders who caused a great deal of trouble for the regular Federal cavalry units stationed near the Maryland border.

With the exception of Solomon's personal exploits, all of the major military events described in the story actually happened. Colonel Dixon Miles, Colonel Benjamin Davis, Major Augustus Corliss, and many of the minor characters were real. Solomon's pivotal role as solitary military scout/artist in this story is fanciful; at least several companies of the Eighth New York Cavalry had crossed the Potomac on scouting missions before the Confederate army arrived. However, the Federal evacuation of Maryland Heights, the argument between Colonel Miles and Colonel Davis, the actual cavalry escape, the capture of the Confederate supply train, and the ultimate surrender of Harpers Ferry all actually happened.

After the campaign, hard questions were asked about the calamity that befell Harpers Ferry. Many soldiers blamed Colonel Dixon Miles, citing everything from mental incompetence to intoxication to outright treason. The War Department quickly appointed a special commission to investigate and determine the causes of the surrender. Forty-four people, primarily military officers but including a few civilians, were questioned. Although most of the officers at Harpers Ferry were not found to be at fault, the commission determined that Colonel Thomas Ford, who had retreated from Maryland Heights, had "...abandoned his position without sufficient cause, and has shown through such a lack of military capacity as to disqualify him... for a command in the service." The commission showed some reluctance to judge the deceased Dixon Miles too harshly, since he was unable to defend himself, but nonetheless concluded that his "incapacity, amounting to almost imbecility, led to the shameful surrender of this important post."

Thanks to the National Park Service, it is possible to visit most of the places described in this story. Many buildings in Harpers Ferry National Historical Park have been preserved, and you can walk along Shenandoah Street where the cavalry lined up for their famous ride. Most of the Union positions targeted during the bombardment were not in the town proper, but further west toward Charles Town in the Bolivar Heights area. Park historians believe Colonel Dixon Miles was fatally wounded somewhere in the vicinity of the modern-day junior high school, near the spot where the garrison was actually surrendered.

If you tour Harpers Ferry look up at Loudon Heights, across the Shenandoah River, and imagine the Confederate gunners wrestling their artillery pieces to the crest. The commanding cliffs of Maryland Heights are also clearly visible, across the Potomac; the fight between Colonel Thomas Ford's Federal troops and the advancing Confederates took place not on those rocky ledges, however, but farther back along the ridge. A footbridge and railroad bridge across the Potomac parallels the place where the pontoon bridge once was, and if you walk down to the shore, you may find ring bolts imbedded in the stone embankments facing the river, believed to be anchors for the original pontoon bridge.

The easiest way to take your tour across the Potomac is to cross on the footbridge, emerging near the remains of Lock Thirty-Three. The white ruin beneath the cliffs is all that remains of Spence's store; the frame addition which housed the tavern (where Solomon met Elisha in this story), as well as other nearby buildings, are gone. The remains are known locally as the Salty Dog Tavern, although that name did not exist during the war.

If you turn right on the towpath when emerging from the bridge you will arrive in the village of Sandy Hook; a left turn will take you toward Lock Thirty-Six. A footbridge across the canal between Lock Thirty-Three and Lock Thirty-Four provides access to a trail leading to the crest of Maryland Heights and Elk Ridge beyond.

The walk to Lock Thirty-Six (less than two miles from Lock Thirty-Three) provides lovely views of the Potomac and Harpers Ferry beyond. Locks Thirty-Five and Thirty-Six were so close together that at times a single lockkeeper tended both, a complexity omitted from this story. The ruins of the house where Mahalia and her family "lived" in this story are still standing, a two-story brick structure largely destroyed during a flood in 1936.